THE BOOK OF
HAROLD
THE ILLEGITIMATE SON OF GOD

THE BOOK OF
HAROLD

THE ILLEGITIMATE SON OF GOD

OWEN EGERTON

Soft Skull Press
An imprint of COUNTERPOINT

Library of Congress Cataloging-in-Publication Data is available.

ISBN: 978-1-59376-438-8

Cover design by Elke Barter
Interior design by Deltina Hay

Soft Skull Press
An imprint of Counterpoint
1919 Fifth Street
Berkeley, CA 94710
www.softskull.com

Distributed by Publishers Group West

10 9 8 7 6 5 4 3 2 1

EGER
18647092
(REF)

To Brad Biggers,
friend and thinker, scarred by faith and a golf cart.

My Rescue, My Capture

"You don't have to jump into the water," I told myself. "Just jump into the air. Gravity will do the rest."

I wavered on the ledge above a stadium-sized reservoir. Beside me stood a flickering florescent streetlight, one of a dozen surrounding the lake like thin, head-heavy soldiers. I watched the oily surface of the water slice the light into a swirl of rainbows. It was time to die, time to drown. After seventy years of living, over thirty of those spent running, I was tired and ready for nothing more. I was coaxing my old, stiff legs to move, when a voice spoke from behind me.

"Mr. Waterson?"

Turning, I saw a group of shadows. They stepped into the ring of light, a dozen polite-looking men in casual slacks and pastel sweaters.

"Blake Waterson, we've come to help you."

I turned back to the water and jumped—a rush of air and then cold, black water. I let myself sink, my shoes and clothes pulling me down. The air bubbled through my mouth and nose, abandoning ship and darting for the surface, making me heavier. Above me there were splashes and voices. The light grew dimmer the deeper I sank and the more water I swallowed. Soon everything was black.

I didn't drown. They didn't let me.

I don't remember being pulled back into the air or having the water squeezed from my chest. I was in the black water and then I woke up here. It's a basement, as far as I can tell. Sparsely furnished. Poorly lit. No windows to the outside. One set of stairs. A door at the top. Locked. There's a cot, a television, a desk where I'm writing now, and a bookshelf filled with Haroldian texts including *An Introduction to Haroldism* by one J.P. Beaman, which I've pulled out and placed on the desk beside my papers. An easel with some paints is set up in a corner, and by the bathroom door stands a foosball table. It feels like the basement of a church, a place for youth group meetings and bible studies.

I don't know what they want from me, my rescuers, my capturers. But judging by the stacks of yellow writing pads and the box of ballpoint pens, I presume they would have me write what I remember. Write my confession. Write about Harold.

BOOK I

Nativity

I never should have been a follower of Harold. That's pretty clear from the history books. I am not a godly man. In truth, God and I have never been on good terms. I've always suspected that perhaps God was hunting me. Not in a good way, not the shepherd searching for a lost sheep. More like a pissed off loan shark looking for payment.

I know it's silly, conceited even, to believe I have the ability to offend the all-powerful monarch of existence. The idea is childish. But I think an event from my childhood explains it.

When I was a young, I believed in God with the same certainty and apathy with which I believed in China. Both were far away and had little to do with my life. I believed in both because I had been told of both. I didn't know not believing in God was an option. God just was.

My family went to church every now and then, and I'd be dropped off in the bright, green and blue Sunday school room. We were irregular attendees, but by chance, in my ninth year, we showed up the day of casting for the live Christmas nativity scene.

This was a Christmas tradition for our church, complete with an outdoor set, a slew of blue and yellow lights, and children dressed up like Romans, Israelites, and angels. A scratched album passed down through the years played the entire story complete with a game-show-announcer-style narration and full-choired carols. All the kids did was mouth along.

Ms. Pock had been directing the nativity for ten years. She was a single woman in her late forties who smelled of hairspray and potpourri. For her the live nativity was as holy as any hymn, any prayer, any stained glass window or Renaissance masterpiece.

Ms. Pock cast most of the second graders as the angelic choir, a handful of fourth graders were assigned the roles of cowering shepherds, one lanky third grader was made King Herod, and the part of Mary was given to a girl named Mary, a coincidence which made the assignment inevitable to all of us. For that year Ms. Pock had also added the role of the Little Drummer Boy.

"But there is no Little Drummer Boy in the Bible," Mary pointed out.

"Oh, yes. He's in there," Ms. Pock answered.

"He's not on the album," Mary said.

"We'll figure something out." She gave the role to her six-year-old nephew, Trevor. I, much to my surprise, was given the role of Joseph. Ms. Pock had forgotten to cast Joseph earlier, and since I hadn't volunteered for any role, I was the only option left.

The star role of Baby Jesus had been portrayed by the same plastic doll for the past decade. Its hair was spotty, one hand had snapped off, and the voice box that mewed "Mamma" each time the doll was lifted had been broken for years. But the Baby Jesus didn't need to cry for Mamma. He was just a swaddled lump to gaze at and occasionally cuddle.

We practiced for the next two weeks. My part was simple enough. I lead a donkey, carrying Mary, to the makeshift stable built in the church parking lot while the album describes our journey from Nazareth to Bethlehem and being turned away at the inn. At this point the focus of the story goes stage left, where shepherds are confronted by angels and told the news. By the time the story returns to the stable, the Baby Jesus has been born, swaddled, and laid to rest in a trough. All I had to do was stand by the trough/crib with Mary and look gooey and fatherly while shepherds and Wise Men visit.

After the record announces the Wise Men's gifts and plays "We Three Kings," Trevor has his big scene. He picks up the microphone which is lying on a bale of hay by the trough and recites the scene's one live line. We had a microphone hooked up just for it.

"Jesus, I am so poor. All I have is a song," was all Trevor had to say. Then he was to place the microphone back on the hay bale beside the sleeping Jesus doll. This gave Ms. Pock just enough time to change records to the *Christmas Classics* album which played "The Little Drummer Boy" while Trevor pretended to play and the rest of us swayed back and forth. At the end of the song, Ms. Pock put the nativity album back on and the show ended with an abbreviated version of Handel's *Messiah* being mouthed by angels dressed in white sheets like hoodless Klan members. Hell of a show.

Trevor did a fine job, except for his one line. He didn't say "Jesus, I am so poor." He said, "Jesus! I am so poor!" Like a low-wage earner taking the savior's name in vain.

The first two nights went fine. A few of the angels cried on night one, and the donkey nibbled on Mary's robe on night two. But the show was a success. People even enjoyed the addition of the Little Drummer Boy.

Our last performance was Christmas Eve. The crowd was the biggest yet, flashing pictures as Mary and I entered from behind the gym. The donkey had been getting grumpier every night and was now protesting his involvement by dropping balls of dung every other step.

That wasn't so bad until a Wise Man approaching the cradle slipped on a dropping and doused the microphone with myrrh. Even that didn't seem so important until the record player went silent and Trevor reached for the wet microphone. "Jesus!" was all he got out. He threw the microphone down and rubbed his hand. The microphone landed right on top of the head of Baby Jesus with a nasty, amplified *bonk*.

For a moment we were all quiet, wondering what to do next, when a miracle happened. The voice box inside Baby Jesus came back to life.

"Mamma," said the Baby Jesus.

The crowd gasped. Jesus had a line. It looked like everything was going to be fine, but then the baby said "Mamma" again. And again. Mary, played by Mary, was too surprised by the change in script to react, so the new mother motionlessly stared down as her child called out for her. On Jesus's fourth "Mamma," the voice box got stuck and the baby wailed one long "Maaaaaaaa." The cry slowed and warped as if Mary had accidentally birthed the Baby Satan. I reached in and tried to move the microphone, but it shocked me. I yanked my hand away, shouting an expletive. I was told later that it looked as if the newborn had snapped at my fingers.

Ms. Pock was desperately trying to get "The Little Drummer Boy" to play, but the album was skipping. "Rum tump. Rum tump. Rum tump. Rum tump." Like a hideous beating heart. Trevor was in tears, holding his hand. Mary still stared into the crib, aghast at the horror she had brought into the world. The Baby Jesus wailed on. The only way to save the show was to shut Jesus up. I tried to shift the doll, knocking it with quick jabs to avoid the microphone. It looked as if I were portraying Joseph as an abusive father. None of it worked. If anything, it seemed the doll was moaning louder. Finally, I picked Jesus up. The sound was coming from somewhere inside the doll's neck. My motives were good, I swear. I wanted things to go smoothly, but my next act was not well-thought-out. With a quick snap, I removed Baby Jesus's head. The crying stopped.

"Holy shit," said one of the shepherds. I heard a child scream from among the onlookers. In one hand I had Jesus's head and in the other his body, quickly unswaddling itself. Even the donkey seemed freaked out. The record player skipped to the next song on the *Christmas Classics* album, which happened to be "Frosty the Snowman." The lights went out and the crowd, unsure what to do, applauded.

In the dark, Mary leaned close to me and whispered, "You're gonna get it."

I never voiced the fear, never even gave it much conscious thought, but ever since that night I've had a sneaking suspicion that I owed God and sooner or later He was going to collect. Years later I met Harold Peeks, well into his thirties, a little thick around the waist, with a half-inch crop of hair—never more, never less—and a goofy, show-it-all grin. I didn't know at the time, but God had finally found me.

Day of Declaration

In the beginning Harold was just a man. Not a particularly exciting man.

We both worked for the Sales and Distribution Department of Promit Computers. I wouldn't have called him a friend. He was simply a face at work, three cubicles down from mine. He lived less than a mile from my family, but I'd never seen him outside of work or work-related events. Harold was the kind of guy I didn't mind comparing myself to because I always came out on top. I was a little younger and fitter. Harold carried a roll of pudge just above his belt. His hair was juvenile, slightly longer than a crew cut, Wally Cleaver all grown up. My hair was dark, thick and wavy, like the hair of a shampoo model.

I sold computers for the Promit company, lots of computers, while Harold, as Second Assistant Sales Analyst, simply analyzed what I was doing. He remained a stationary figure on the corporate ladder, neither competition for promotions nor a butt I had to kiss to get one. Harold couldn't help me or hurt me, so we got along fine.

I worked hard at Promit Computers and I was good at what I did. For three years running, I won Highest Sales Achiever at the annual Employees' Banquet.

Ah, those banquets. Always the same dry chicken, soggy broccoli, and watered-down iced tea. Each year the same speeches designed to encourage and entertain and failing on both fronts. But I liked the awards. I liked the vice president of the company smiling as he shook my hand. I liked being told I was doing a good job.

At my last banquet at Promit Computers, they hung up a banner saying:

We're not just selling computers. We're selling the future!

I liked that. I was helping to create the future.

I sat at a round table with my wife, daughter, and half a dozen co-workers. We laughed at office inside jokes and talked about baseball. My wife, Jennifer, discussed granite kitchen counters with the woman to her left. My daughter, Tammy, text-messaged her friends. She would study the scene every now and then, quickly type a message, and giggle her well-practiced teenage giggle, high-pitched and superior.

"What's so funny?" I whispered to her. She shook her head and went back to typing.

The awards came: Employee of the Year, Best Time-to-Sell Ratio, Highest Sales Achiever. I walked up, collected my plaque, and shook the aging vice president's hand. My wife smiled and clapped. My daughter never looked up from her phone.

Towards the end of the evening, they moved on to less prestigious awards: Most Punctual Employee, Cleanest Cubicle. People were starting to sneak out, leaving their dollop of rainbow sherbet melting at the table. I was trying to gather my family and do the same.

"We better get going," I explained to my co-workers. "Tammy's got a load of homework."

"No I don't, Dad."

"Well," I said, "it's late," and pushed my chair back.

"Our next award is for Most Improved Sales Analyst," the company vice president announced, smoothing down his well-gelled comb-over. "It goes to Harold Peeks."

Harold stood from his table just as I was standing from mine. He smiled at me, looking pleasantly surprised. He was thirty-nine then, had been with the company almost as long as me and, as far as I knew, had never been recognized at any banquet before. He walked to the podium amidst a smattering of applause as I pulled Tammy to her feet.

"Geez, Dad. I'm coming, okay?"

Harold took the plaque and shook the VP's hand. I herded my family to the door and nodded a few goodbyes. Then, as the vice president turned around to pick up the next award, Harold stepped behind the podium.

"Thank you for the honor, but I'm not sure if I should receive it," he said. "I do have an unfair advantage since I am Christ, the Son of God. But thank you all the same."

There were a few nervous chuckles, a few cleared throats. Harold Peeks walked back to his seat, leaving the plaque on the podium. The vice president, who apparently had been too busy with the next award to hear the speech, continued with the presentations. I shook my head and left.

An Introduction to Haroldism
Day of Declaration

On September 2 believers around the world celebrate the Day of Declaration with a feast of chicken, broccoli, and iced tea. During the meal, a predetermined member of the group will stand before the feasters to ask them three questions.

Q: Why do we eat this meal?
A: Because he ate this meal.

Q: Why is the chicken dry and the broccoli limp?
A: Because our hearts were dry and our faith was limp.

Q: What has changed?
A: Hope has come. Harold has come. Life is sweet again.

The feast is then completed with bowls of rainbow sherbet and awards for the children.

The Office Miracle

This all happened over thirty-two years ago, before the Collapse, before Haroldism. I was thirty-eight then. I felt mature and established. In hindsight, I was practically a child.

When I arrived at work the day after the banquet, I noticed the banner.

We're not just selling computers. We're selling the future!

It was now hanging over the windows at the far end of the cubicles.

I hadn't been at the office ten minutes before the under-vice president called me in to see him.

"Blake, I need you to fire somebody," he told me. Firing people was an unofficial part of my job at Promit Computers. And I liked it. It had more of a punch than making phone calls and sending emails. "It's Peeks. Last night was totally fucking inappropriate. Not funny."

"I agree."

"But don't tell him that's the reason, or we'll have some fucking right to free fucking religion or free speech or something on our ass. Take him to lunch. Do it gently."

"Fine."

"Hell, we were going to fire him next quarter anyway. Him and half the building. Fucking pessimistic board and their cutbacks." He paused and looked up at me. "That's between you and me, Blake. Understood?"

"Of course."

I left the U.V.P.'s office and made my way through the cubicles. I found Harold sitting on his swivel chair, staring at the cream spinning in his coffee. He looked weak.

"Hey friend, want to grab lunch?"

He looked up and his eyes were dark, hollow, as if he'd been staring into his coffee for hours. It took him a moment to adjust his focus. He smiled.

"It's a lie, you know," he said, motioning with eyes to the banner. "We are just selling computers."

"Sure." I laughed a little, as if he were making a joke. "Lunch?"

He nodded and went back to staring at his coffee.

Stella's, one my favorite downtown Houston restaurants, was only two blocks from the office. But a Houston August is sick with heat. Sweat-salt stains your shirt within moments of stepping outside. You're forced to dash from climate controlled building to climate controlled building like fish hopping from puddle to puddle. My father used to say that before air conditioning was readily available, August would be a month of melting. Not just lawn furniture or ice cream, people would melt. The heat would melt minds, dissolve marriages, liquefy businesses. As my father put it, "Too hot to give a damn."

Finally, we reached Stella's and stepped into the cold, pumping air. They sat us next to one of the wall-sized tinted windows facing the sidewalk. We made small talk, gave our orders. You can't tell someone they're fired at the beginning of the meal and expect to eat comfortably. So you talk about the menu, last night's baseball game, the restaurant's glass walls. You avoid office gossip or business talk—since that's the circle they're being removed from. By the time I'm asking them out for lunch, the person usually knows what's coming. But they play along, patiently waiting through a crab salad and grilled trout with asparagus sauce.

With Harold the small talk was difficult. He still had those coffee eyes. His face was tense, as if he was trying to remember something. He chewed slowly, sometimes coming to a complete stop. More than once, I think he forgot there was food in his mouth at all.

"Harold, I'm afraid I've got some bad news." I started my little speech but he was hardly listening. "As you know the company has been making some cutbacks."

"Blake, would you excuse me for a moment?" He walked off before I could say another word. I checked my watch. This was taking longer than I planned. Ten minutes passed and no Harold. I got the bill and paid it. One of the perks of these firing-lunches was that the company picked up the bill. Fifteen minutes and I began to wonder if Harold was crying in the bathroom or already on his way home. I started scanning the restaurant. Then I saw him by the door. He wasn't wearing a shirt. He was walking back to our table, all eyes watching him, his tiny pink nipples aimed directly at me.

"Harold, what happened?"

"Oh, kind of a silly story." He sat down calmly. "So you were saying something about cutbacks?"

A waiter dashed over to our table. "Excuse me, sir," he whispered. "We have a clothing policy. You'll have to leave."

I quickly stood up, took off my jacket and wrapped it around Harold. "I'm so sorry, really sorry," I told the waiter.

"He's also in violation of our footwear policy," the waiter said, eyebrows rising. I looked down at Harold's feet as I pulled him from his chair. Sure enough, no shoes, no socks. I dragged him out of the restaurant.

"What the hell, Harold?" I said once we were walking. "I have a reputation in that place. I like being there, and now . . ." Harold wasn't with me. I turned around and saw him half a block back talking to a bum with a matted gray and black beard. But the bum was wearing a clean white shirt, a brown suit jacket, and a pair of leather dress shoes. Harold said something and the bum started laughing. A loud, long laugh.

"Harold!" I yelled. Harold turned to me and waved. Then he shook the bum's hand and jogged in my direction.

"How about that restaurant?" he said as he reached me. "Pretty uptight, huh?"

"Harold, you're fired."

"That's okay. I quit." He handed me my jacket, once again exposing his pasty chest to the world. "When are *you* going to quit, Blake?"

"I'm not," I told him, picking up my pace, hoping he'd fall behind. But he kept up.

"You should," he said. His bare feet slapping, somehow managing the heat of the pavement. "It's not your vocation."

Back in the office no one mentioned Harold's appearance. He walked to his cube under the side-glances of his fellow workers and cheerfully packed his things. I sat in my own cubicle, rocking in my chair, letting the anger and embarrassment recede. My cubicle had soft, gray walls. In the middle of one wall was an older picture of my wife and daughter stuck up with a thumbtack. They're standing on a white beach wearing matching yellow bathing suits. The photo is like a small window in the side of the cubicle. Sometimes I glance out and see my wife and child standing very far away. I was looking at them when Harold, still shirtless, popped his head into my cubicle.

"Bye, Blake."

"Bye, Harold," I said. He started to go, but I stopped him. "Harold, why did you give that man your clothes?"

"I asked him what he wanted and that's what he wanted."

"Why did he laugh like that?"

"I told him what he really wanted."

"What was that?"

"None of your concern, Blake." He disappeared behind the wall. "See you soon."

I stood up and watched him walk down the aisle, past three rows, and out the large glass doors. The doors slowly closed behind him. The moment they clicked shut every wall of every cubicle collapsed. Thirty-five faces all stared at each other as if the door of their bathroom stall had vanished.

It was the first miracle I witnessed.

Sand

Home was like sand. I could hardly walk through the front door without feeling it fill my lungs, clog my ears, seal up the corners of my eyes, and muffle everything. My sad wife and angry daughter were in that sand somewhere too. Each night we moved in labored steps from the TV, to the dinner table, to the TV, to bed, to sleep. Every word and action painfully predictable.

As I walked in that evening, my daughter Tammy was standing on the stairs and once again yelling at my wife.

"I'm a sophomore. They're building the sophomore float. I have to be there!"

"Well, you should have thought about that before."

Painfully predictable and sand. Even the yelling hardly reached me. Tammy gave one final scream, ran up the remaining steps, and slammed her bedroom door. My wife Jennifer turned to me. "I don't care if she yells herself hoarse, I really don't," she said, rubbing her knuckles with the palm of her hand, a habit of hers since college. "She hasn't even started her history paper." She closed her eyes and took a long, deliberate breath. "Okay, okay," she said in a whisper. She opened her eyes and smiled at me. "Let's check in."

Let's check in was a gift from our marriage counselor, Patricia Watts. Twice over the past six months we had visited Patricia, a thin woman in her fifties with dark brown cow eyes. On our first visit, we sat before her desk in a rose-scented office, nervously waiting for her to diagnose the health of our relationship. She studied us with those round eyes and said, "Before we dive in, I have a question. It's the question I ask of all couples who come to see me. The question is this: do you *really want* to save your marriage?"

"Yes!" I said quickly. Too quickly. I knew it. Jennifer knew it. I answered quickly to close the question. If the question were open I would have to consider it. If I had to consider it at all, then what kind of hope did we have? How valuable can something be if you're not sure whether you want it or not? Uncertainty was judgment, like clearing the leftovers from the fridge: "When in doubt, throw it out."

Before we left that day, Patricia Watts had us hold hands and look into each other's eyes. "Good. Now at the end of each day, or whenever you feel you need it, hold hands and share three things about your day. Anything at all. Just *checking in*."

I looked at my wife in our foyer. I could see middle age creeping across her face like mold across cheese. Her skin was dry, lines splaying from the corners of her eyes. Her hair, once a light gold, was now the fading brown of sun-baked pine needles.

"I finished the novel for the book club. The one about the Jewish girl and the music box. Really wonderful. It made me cry. I want you to read it. I ordered flowers for my mother's birthday. She won't like them, but she'll be mad if I don't send them. And, let's see, Pickles got out this afternoon. I'm sure he'll wander back." She sighed and squeezed my hands. "Your turn."

"I can only think of one."

"It's supposed to be three. Anything counts."

"Okay. I ate lunch at Stella's."

"See, that works."

"I didn't close the Blackstone account. But it feels close."

She nodded.

"And I fired that Peeks guy. Harold Peeks."

"Do I know him?"

"Maybe. He—"

Upstairs a stereo clicked and hammered bass through the ceiling and down on our heads. Jennifer's smile disappeared and more lines shattered across her forehead.

"Tammy!" my wife yelled. The music was notched up a few decimals louder. "I tell you, Blake, she's driving me nuts."

I thought about telling Jennifer about the bum and the clothes and the cubicles, but instead I patted her back and said, "She's just going through a phase." I trudged through the sand to fix myself a drink. Painfully predictable.

"The guests will be here in less than half an hour. Are you going to change?"

I'd forgotten. The dinner party.

"The Miltons backed out," my wife called. "So it's just the Klotters and the Williamsons."

I poured my gin, added my tonic, hoping I could wash some of the sand out of my throat. People struggle and fight, but they're just trying to move in the sand. You try all you can, but the screams and slamming doors are all muffled. You get used to it, resigned to the fact that you're powerless, caught in the sand. You even grow bold, believing you can't affect anything. So you raise the ax high above your head and the sand drains away in an instant and everything moves at superspeed and all your actions have enormous, irreversible consequences and there's an affair or a bruised child or a car crash and you feel tricked. But no one will listen, or they pretend they don't understand, when you ask, "Why does it count this time?"

I clicked on the flat screen television that hung on our living room wall and was about to sit and lose myself in gin and football highlights when a knock came from the front door. My wife had already disappeared into the kitchen, so I slogged to the foyer and opened the door. There stood Harold and my dog Pickles.

Another Miracle

"I found him wandering," Harold said. "He was on Maple, near my house."

I was going to ask how he knew it was my dog, but Jennifer showed up behind me with *thank yous* and *won't you please come ins*.

"I thought he'd just wander back," my wife laughed, touching Harold's arm. "We're having some people over for dinner, and my mind is gone. You know Blake from work?"

"That's true, yes," Harold said with a smile, Pickles sticking to his calf, a fat, squat, pepper-haired bodyguard.

Jennifer had a soft spot for lost mutts. That's how we got Pickles. Found him as a puppy wandering around a construction site. It was Harold's lost puppy look that got him an invite to dinner as well. "Why don't you join us?" Jennifer asked. "We have an empty spot."

Of course, it was customary to turn down such invitations, but Harold never cared much for custom. "I'd absolutely love to." My wife directed him into the living room. He walked on, Pickles waddling beside him.

I grabbed Jennifer's elbow and held her back.

"Why'd you do that?" I asked.

"It was the polite thing to do."

"I fired him today," I said through my teeth.

"All the more reason to show him kindness," she said, looking at me as if I were crazy. I wanted to tell her that it was Harold who was crazy, not me, but she was following Harold into the next room. Harold was staring at the television, sport scores flashing across the screen. Pickles curled up beside my big leather chair.

"You two boys entertain yourselves, I've still got a salad to toss!"

And there we were. Harold smiling. Me not smiling.

"Drink?" I asked.

"Do you have any Amarula?"

I scowled.

"It's a cream liquor made from the marula fruit of Africa."

"No, Harold. I don't have any Amarula."

"It's delicious."

"Hmm."

"Nice television," he said, stepping towards the flat screen.

"Thanks," I said. "Got it last—"

Harold placed an open palm on the screen. A quiet pop and the television blinked to black.

"What did you do?"

"I think it's broken," he said.

"No shit it's broken!" I was clicking on the remote but the screen was dead.

The doorbell rang. The guests. The dinner party. I downed my drink and went for the door.

The Pickles Miracle

There were the Klotters and the Williamsons, both full of smiles and compliments on how nice the house looked. Terry Williamson, a broad man with a head full of red curls, slapped my back and handed me a bottle of white wine.

"Let's begin with some lubrication, huh?" he said and laughed like a middle-aged Santa.

I pushed my aggravation out my head and started pouring drinks and my wife brought out the appetizers. Harold stood nodding and smiling with each introduction.

The dinner party began, and as always, it was as if a game were commencing. We could have called it *Dinner in a Deck*, a must-own for any social gathering.

The directions were easy to follow. As the guests arrive, the host hands out stacks of Conversation Cards, each with its own line of dialogue.

Some cards have straightforward lines:

—*What a lovely home you have.*

—*Have you done something with your hair?*

Others are multiple choice:

—*The weather lately has been so (a. pleasant b. rainy c. unseasonal).*

—*Did you hear about ___ and ___? They're (a. having a baby b. getting a divorce c. both a. & b.).*

If you're playing for points, as we almost always were, there was a scoring method. For example, if one player uses the card reading:

—*We're thinking of going to ___ next year. We hear it's beautiful.*

Another player can counter with the card reading:

—*Ah, yes. We went there once, but it isn't as nice as ___ (more expensive destination).*

Improvisation is discouraged, but if attempted, there are some ground rules:

Arguments should be limited to subjects one cannot in any way affect, i.e. sports or the decisions of television characters.

Controversial statements about politics or religion may only be made if the speaker is sure the other players will all agree with the statement.

Repetition of former conversations is encouraged.

Avoid silence at all cost.

The object of the game is to keep the game going.

Once a group, like ours, reaches a certain level of skill, the cards can be abandoned. We knew our lines, understood our roles, and could safely improvise.

But then there was Harold. He didn't know the game at all. Or, if he did, he was refusing to play it. I was embarrassed for him. He didn't laugh at Terry Williamson's jokes. He didn't congratulate Rebecca Klotter on her new earrings. He didn't nod along when Rick Klotter solemnly announced, "No matter what, we support the troops. That's priority one."

He had never been snow skiing—lost points.

He wasn't married—lost points.

Harold didn't have a job—lost points.

At first he was a curiosity, then a joke, but after a while he became a threat. Beth Williamson was remarking on an article about plastic surgery, how it was safe and many younger women were having it done.

"A bit like cutting off your ears so you won't hear the thunder," Harold said through a mouth of food.

Beth's expression looked as if she were smelling something south of foul.

"With the stress of the market these days, we're all going to need a little work done. Am I right?" Terry said. The room laughed, even Beth, and the game continued.

"Anyone like dessert?" my wife asked.

Later, I wandered into the living room. Pickles was there, a furry ball on the carpet by the leather chair. I expected him to wake up and shuffle off to a quieter place, but he didn't budge.

"Go on, out you go," I told him. He still didn't move. "Okay, Pickles, wake up," I said and gave him a little kick. He shifted in one solid hunk and with a painful jab I realized that Pickles was not going to wake up. Not now, not ever.

I thought about moving the dog or hiding it, but the men meandered in behind me. The women soon followed. None of them noticed anything. Which is good. Nothing ruins a party like a dead dog.

"Anyone want a nightcap?" I asked, making my way to the bar. And the game continued.

. . . I sure hope this summer isn't as hot as . . . sixteen-year-old Wendy going to Europe alone? I think not. Of course cheerleading camp has taught

*her how to . . . hunt quail in Mexico. It has twice the adventure of hunting
. . . Democrats! They don't understand a working man's. . .implants. I
mean, they can't be real . . .*

Talk away, keep it up. Never mind the dog. Everything is A-Okay.

When I came back with drinks, I found Terry Williamson sitting in
the leather chair next to Pickles's corpse. He sat there smiling with his
ruddy cheeks aglow. He casually dropped his hand to scratch behind
Pickles's ear. His fingers just brushed the dog's skin when he yanked
his hand away with a gasp. Only I saw him. He looked at me, just a tad
horrified. But he said nothing. Keep the game going.

I sat rubbing my hands. If they knew, they would cry. I wanted to
cry, and I didn't like the dog that much. Jennifer would be worst of all
and the game would stop. I noticed Rebecca Klotter quietly whistling
for the dog. "Rebecca," I said. "Would you like another drink?"

"No, thanks," she said and continued with her cooing. A touch of
doubt was sneaking into her whistled melody.

"Are you sure you don't want a drink, Rebecca?" She looked up.
Our eyes met. Maybe it was my face that told her, maybe it was the fact
that the dog hadn't responded to any of her calls, maybe it was the fly
that was crawling along the dog's dry nose. Whatever it was, Rebecca
now knew Pickles was no longer with us. I shook my head at her and
glanced quickly at my wife. Rebecca nodded and leaned back in her
chair. Keep the game going.

*. . . If I told her once I told her a hundred times, don't . . . taste as
good as the fat-free ones. The fatty ones always . . . get the girls. You have
a means of support, a charming personality . . . an infected bladder. The
doctor says it's most likely due to . . . Pickles—*

It was my wife speaking.

"Pickles loves to chase those squirrels. He even dreams about it.
Watch him. Any minute now his little legs will start running in midair.
It is so cute."

Rebecca looked at me. I looked at her. Terry looked at me. I looked
at him. Then we all looked at the dog. Fourteen eyes fixated on the
furry little body.

No one talked, just watched, but the legs were not moving. If
anything, they looked a little stiff. Rigor mortis must have been setting
in. The seconds ticked by and the dog didn't stir. Not a twitch or
postmortem shudder. Nothing. Another fly landed on Pickles's closed
eye. Still nothing. Just when I was sure my wife and the others would
catch on, Terry spoke up.

"Oh, there it went. A little hop." He slapped his knee.

"He hopped?" my wife asked.

"Oh, yeah. The dream squirrel must be up a dream tree." We all laughed and quickly looked away from the corpse. If people in that room still thought the dog was alive, it was only because they were willing to be deceived. We continued chuckling at Terry's little joke and kept our eyes up.

I took a swallow of my drink. When I drew the glass away from my face, I saw Harold was staring at me.

"A woman in Paris just killed her two children," Harold said.

"What?"

"Since we finished dinner, two hundred and seven people have starved to death. The sun has risen on seven percent of the globe. At this moment, three blocks from here, a grandfather is describing what a whale looks like to his granddaughter. I've always been afraid of possums."

"Harold, what are you—"

"A woman in Boston is using coal to sketch her husband's face. My mother used to call me Huck. She loved Mark Twain. A man in Africa is being shot in the head for a crime he did not commit. He wants his daughter to know he's innocent."

"Okay, let's quit the dramatics."

"One hundred and four people are dying this minute. Two hundred and fifty-three are being born. Over seven billion people are alive and kicking. And that dog is dead."

"What?" my wife cried.

"Ah, honey, he's not. He's fine," I said. My wife fell to the floor and shook Pickles. I had been right about the rigor mortis. Beth moved to her side and put an arm around my wife's shoulders.

"That was heartless, Harold," Terry said.

"You'd rather her not know?"

"Show some compassion, for Christ's sake."

"That's exactly whose sake I do it for," Harold said.

"Really? You speak for Christ?"

"Of course I do. I am Christ."

Game over. Claim you're the Messiah, the game ends. It's so obvious they left it out of the rule book.

"Look, Mr. Peeks," said Beth from my wife's side, "I find that kind of joke very offensive."

"It's more offensive than that," Harold said. "I wasn't joking."

"I promise you, you are not Jesus."

"No, you're right. I'm Harold," he nodded. "But I am Christ, Son of God."

"Okay, that's enough," Terry said.

"Things are fine, things are fine," my wife said tearfully, still kneeling in front of Pickles's body. "I'll make coffee. Who wants coffee?"

"You're wasting time, and you're wasting words," Harold said. "How many hours have you spent together? You know nothing about each other. Beth, you've never told them about your first child. Rick, you've—"

"How do you know . . ." Beth stuttered.

"Now wait just one minute, this is inappropriate," Rick said, rising to his feet.

"No, this is what language is for. You've forgotten how to talk. How can you talk of anything real if you can't mention that a dog is dead?" He turned to Jennifer. "I'm sorry about your loss. I'll leave now."

"Yes," said Rick. "I think that's best."

My scowling guests, my weeping wife, Harold moving to leave—I started to snicker. It started small, a muffled chuckle, but it quickly grew into a loud, big belly laugh. Terry smiled, laughed a little himself and asked, "Was this some kind of practical joke, Blake?"

"No," I said. "The dog's dead, and he says he's the Son of God. No joke." I was laughing so hard I had to stand and lean on my chair. I looked over at Harold with his cropped hair and round face, his big eyes and wrinkled clothes. Tears started welling in my eyes.

"I don't see what's so funny, Blake," Rebecca said. At first I couldn't answer because of the laughing, but finally I squeezed out, "What if it's true?"

"Oh, please."

"I mean, look at him. That's our savior?" I couldn't stop my laughing. "And we're all ready to crucify him because he said the dog is dead and ruined the party. Quick, get me a cross! We can do it right now. Who's with me?" I was laughing and yelling.

Husbands were putting jackets on wives, all glaring at me. My poor wife was apologizing and wiping away her tears, and I was still laughing. The more seriously they stared, the more I saw the absurdity. My guests were absurd, my wife was absurd, I was definitely absurd, and Harold was the most absurd of us all.

I tried to follow my guests and wave goodbye, but I was laughing so much I stumbled and stepped on Pickles. He let out a bark.

We all stopped and stared. I gave him a little kick to see if he would move. He didn't. He was still dead. I started laughing again.

Within two minutes everyone but Harold had left. My wife was shaking from embarrassment and grief. Harold took a step towards her and put a hand on her arm. My wife spun away. "Please go," she said.

He nodded.

I stopped laughing and watched Harold walk out the door.

My Prayer for Pickles

I say a prayer for Pickles,
First of the martyrs.
First of the new saints.
Good dog.

I say a prayer for Pickles,
Dog of the Disciple,
Dog of the Destroyer.
Poor dog.

Say a prayer for Pickles.

It Would Have Been Wiser to Say Nothing at All

I was on the couch drinking a gin and tonic when my daughter crept through the front door.

"You're late," I said.

"No, I'm not."

I didn't know if she was late or not. It just seemed like the right thing to say. Painfully predictable. She stood there for a moment and then moved for the stairs.

"Don't go in the garage, okay?" I said. She stopped and turned back to me.

"Why?"

"Just don't."

"Where's Pickles?" she asked.

"In the garage."

She walked off. I could hear the door to the garage open. Pickles was laying in a cooler, covered in a pile of ice. I expected a scream or yelp from Tammy, but there was nothing. After a moment I heard the door click shut. When I looked up again she was standing in the foyer staring at me. I stared at my drink. From the corner of my eye I could see her. Tall for her age and thin. Angry. The way her arms hung heavy from her shoulders, an overstuffed purse dangling like a sandbag from one hand. Angry. The way her chin pointed to the floor. Angry. Even her perfume smelled angry. She didn't say a word. Just stared.

"I had nothing to do with it," I said. I got up and went to join my sad wife in bed.

My Daughter

I should explain about Tammy. She once caught me drowning a cat. Not an adult cat. A kitten, a newborn with its eyes still closed. A nasty, rust-colored cat that my daughter predictably named Rusty Cat used to haunt our neighborhood. It had a litter of six deranged, scratching little beasts. I found them in our garage in a box behind my wife's college bicycle. Feral things, not an hour out of the womb and already spitting away. Their mother, Rusty Cat, was still warm, but dead next to the litter. The kindest thing I could do for the kittens and the neighborhood was to drown the little bastards.

I filled a bathroom sink with water, warm enough to feel like going back into the womb. I picked out one of them, placed it in the sink, and held it down. At first, it just lay there without moving. Then it struggled and scratched, but I was wearing gloves. After a minute or so, the fight was over and it was still. I picked it out of the sink, heavier now, and tossed it in a garbage bag. Then I moved on to the next kitten.

Tammy came in just as I was finishing up the second to last. She screamed. I explained about going back into the womb and the closed eyes and the dead mother, and Tammy screamed again. Then she grabbed the last kitten, a rusty one like its mother, and ran. She was only seven at the time, but she outran me. Down the hall, through the kitchen, around the dinner table, and out the front door. I followed, hoping to explain that my intentions were kind, but I couldn't find her. When I finally returned to the bathroom, the garbage bag and the dead kittens it held were gone. I didn't find out where until the next morning. Five tiny graves now lay in the corner of our backyard, complete with miniature crosses. In a fit of self-righteousness, Tammy dubbed the surviving kitten MLK. It managed to endure thanks to blankets and milk bottles from my daughter, and it quickly grew to be as much of a disease-carrying menace as its mother.

Tammy never forgave me. I think she judged everything I said or did from then on in light of that day's events. If I made dinner, it was the Cat Killer making dinner. If I drove her to school, it was the Cat Killer driving her to school. If I gave her a gift, it was a gift from the Cat Killer. She wouldn't even ask me for money. She would only ask her mother, as if perhaps my money had come directly from the evil profession of cat killing.

Peter Doesn't

I don't feel well. I'm dying. They stopped me from drowning, but my lungs soaked in enough water. So instead of two minutes, it will take two weeks.

A young man named Peter visits the basement three times a day. I watch him carefully. He unlocks and locks the door. He brings me food and extra notepads. He has a serious face and gray eyes. The men who pulled me from the reservoir—who now peak at me through the window in the door—wear pastel sweaters and small silver pins in the shape of the number four. Today Peter wears a white buttoned shirt, well-starched.

In the corner of the basement, near the easel, I found poster prints of masterpieces: Van Gogh, Gauguin.

"Could you tape these posters to the wall?" I asked Peter.

"Yes," he said.

"Can I read the books?" I asked, though I'd already started.

"Yes."

"Can I use the paints and easel?"

"Anything. We don't care." He turned to leave.

"Wait, will you take the TV away?"

"I don't even think it works."

"Of course it doesn't. Will you please take it away?"

Peter lugged the television up the stairs and out the door.

"Thank you," I said. He grunted. I don't think he likes me.

I have very little theology left in me, but I do know that God and Satan are at war in the televisions of America.

Perfectly Folded

The morning after our dinner party, I woke feeling panic like pebbles in my blood. I lay motionless in my bed, unable to think of a reason to rise. Jennifer called me downstairs for breakfast and I was thankful for the distraction. Jennifer and I ate eggs and toast in silence, the events of the previous night willfully ignored. Tammy was still asleep or hiding in her room.

I checked on Pickles. He was still there, stiff under a thin cover of ice cubes. I loaded the cooler into the trunk of my car and dialed up our veterinarian. Closed. I called another. Closed. I called the humane society.

"Oh, we're closed for the weekend."

"But I'm talking to you."

"Yep, I'm here. But I'm not working."

"You're just hanging out?"

I added another handful of ice to the cooler and left it in the trunk.

I fell onto the couch, clicked the remote three or four times before remembering that my television was as dead as my dog.

The panic rumbled. There was nothing I had to do and nothing I wanted to do. Then it hit me: there's always yard work. I gathered my tools like a warrior selecting weapons and set out to perfect my backyard. I cleaned the pool and fixed a loose fence board. For a time it felt good, like I was accomplishing something, doing my duty. I did a once-over on the riding lawn mower—zigzag, zigzag. But the grass on the left side seemed a little taller than the right side. So I rode over that side again. Now the right side looked higher. Another round. I missed a patch. I made a patch. Another round. My shirt was drenched with sweat and pieces of cut grass were sticking to the back of my neck. Whenever I turned around, I found an uneven patch of grass and I'd attack it with the mower. In some spots the soil was beginning to show through. And then there were those five graves in the corner. Unsightly lumps much bigger than the kittens I had drowned. They must have grown under my lawn. Now they were full-sized cat corpses.

What now? What now? What now? What now?

"Honey," Jennifer's voice called from inside, "can you take Tammy to the mall?"

Sweet deliverance.

I gathered my angry daughter and a sulky friend and drove them to the mall.

"You can just drop us off, Dad," Tammy whined as I maneuvered into a parking space.

"I've actually got some shopping to do."

"But Dad, look at you."

I looked at me. I was still dressed for yard work. Gym shorts, a white undershirt stained with rings of dried sweat and smears of soil and my worn out sneakers tearing at the seams.

"I look fine."

The girls shot off, promising to call when they were ready to leave. I walked through the glass doors alone.

Peace—clean, white-tiled hallways with towering ceilings that echoed happy chatter. With slow steps, I explored. Stores lining the hallway like side-chapels, genderless mannequins staring out like saints. Fountains and atriums, music floating from somewhere far above. It was beautiful.

I stepped into a store called Safari. Immediately, a pretty young girl approached me and asked, "May I help you?"

Someone wanted to help me. It struck me as if I'd never heard the phrase before.

"There's a sale on men's shirts," she said.

Within twenty minutes, I walked away with a button-down blue cotton shirt, loose-fit khaki pants, and a black belt, all perfectly folded and packed into my very own Safari bag.

Before long I found myself stepping into a store called The Stop. It had pastel columns and posters of fantastically sculpted men and women.

"May I help you?"

In another twenty minutes I left with another button-down blue cotton shirt, another pair of loose-fit khaki pants, and another black belt, all perfectly folded and packed into my very own The Stop bag.

Next came Froner & Co.

Then Zondee's.

Then Crash Course.

Then New Crop.

I was trying to disentangle the smells of the food court when my cell phone rang and my daughter informed me that she was ready to go. I collected my bags and went to meet them.

"Oh my God, Dad! What did you get?" Tammy asked.

"Just some clothes." I smiled, but already the pebbles were once again rolling through my veins. We walked out to the car, the girls ahead and me behind, waddling with my bags. "Red car, blue car, green car, my car."

"He's just trying to be funny," my angry daughter told her sulking friend.

Stay, Stay

A mile from our house I pulled to the side of the road and told the girls to stay in the car.

"Dad! What are you doing?"

I popped the trunk and grabbed the blue cooler. It felt heavier now. The weight sloshed around as I heaved it to the curb. Then I pulled out my cell.

"Yeah, Waste Control?" It was a machine. I left a message. "There's a roadkill over on Shepherds Drive. Near the Texaco. Thanks."

I wanted to leave him in the cooler, but they'd never find him. So with a kick, I dumped the cooler—dog, water, and ice. Pickles rolled out—wet and stiff like some corpse floating up from the Titanic. *Stay. Stay.*

I threw the cooler back in the trunk and climbed behind the wheel.

"What were you doing?" my daughter asked in a slow, quiet voice.

"Public service," I said and turned on the radio.

Released

Once home, I disappeared to my room and carefully unpacked my treasures. I pushed the old clothes down the rack to make room for the new. I sat on the bed and watched them hang—so still, so sure of themselves. What now? What now? What now?

"Dinner in ten!" my wife called. Thank you, God.

I came downstairs and fixed myself a drink.

Jennifer wanted to *check in*. "Let's see, I restocked the freezer. We were nearly out of everything. I still need to make another run. I finally organized our photos from the ski trip. That took a while. And Rebecca called. We talked about last night and Pickles and your friend. I told her you had fired him, and she said it was lucky he didn't come over with a gun. It happens. So, that was my day." She squeezed my hands. "Now you."

"I mowed the lawn, I bought some clothes, I fixed a gin and tonic."

"That's it?"

"I did three."

Jennifer waited a moment. Then nodded and released my hands.

I opened a bottle of wine. Drinky drinky stop the thinky.

My daughter's sulky friend stayed for dinner and the four of us gathered round the table for twice-baked potatoes and awkward silence. Jennifer filled the space with questions for the friend: How were classes? Was she taking driver's ed? When are musical tryouts?

I asked a question too. "Would you rather be burned at the stake or buried alive?"

"Excuse me?" The friend giggled nervously.

"Blake!" my wife said, banging her fork to her plate.

"It's a good question. A person needs to know these things."

"You're drunk, Dad."

"Not yet," I said, pouring the last of the wine.

"That's not funny." Tammy's face was red. "You're not funny."

"Now, Tammy," Jennifer started. But Tammy jumped to her feet.

"It's true, Mom. He drinks too much."

"Maybe you don't drink enough," I said. To this day I believe that to be the dumbest thing I've ever said. Tammy grunted and ran from the room. Jennifer followed. I stood, the room moving around me. I took my drink and walked to the patio door.

"Buried," the friend said, still sitting at the table. "If you're buried, there's a chance someone could find you."

I nodded my approval and stepped outside.

The pool water wrinkled in the night breeze and cast blue ripples onto the side of the house. I watched, sipping my wine. The blue, the pool, the night—all sufficiently blurry. I tried to calm my head, ease my blood. I walked to the side of the pool and touched the surface with my foot, wondering if it could, if it would, hold me. Why shouldn't it hold me? It should. I took a deep breath and stepped. I sank like a stone. Under the water the world was even blurrier and the chlorine stung my eyes. That was my baptism. Dunked in failure.

I was in bed when my wife came in the room from the shower. She sagged. Everything about her sagged, her face, her breasts, her stomach, all slinking to the floor in a slow spill.

She crawled into her side of the bed. "Did you go in the pool?" she asked.

"No," I said.

"Oh," she said and not another word. My hair was wet, I smelled like chlorine, the sheets were damp—of course, I had been in the pool, of course, I had just lied, but she wouldn't challenge it. I wanted her to accuse me of lying, just once to tell me she knew I was lying. Instead, she switched off the light. We lay quiet in the dark.

"I'm going to stop drinking," I said.

"Okay," she said.

Lump on the Lump

The next morning I woke early and quickly dressed. Work would be a relief. An escape from questions like, "What do you want?"

I was tightening my tie when Jennifer rolled over and stared at me with sleepy eyes.

"Honey," she said through a yawn. "It's Sunday."

I stopped tightening the tie. I took off the suit and got back into bed.

What now? What now? What now?

I had sex with my wife. It was a sad, clumsy episode. Thankfully, it didn't last long. Then I was sitting on the edge of the bed feeling sick with Jennifer running her hand down my back.

Downstairs, I found the automatic coffeemaker making coffee. The yard looked like a prison haircut, the television was still broken, and I wanted nothing. So I went back to bed. But by the time I got upstairs, my wife was already gathering the sheets in a ball and throwing them into the laundry basket. The bed was dead.

I dressed in a button-down blue cotton shirt, loose-fit khaki pants and black belt and sat in front on my broken television.

Tammy went to a friend's house. Jennifer went shopping for groceries. The house was mine. I thought of the homeless man and Harold telling him what he *really* wanted. What did I want? Really want. I *really* wanted a drink, but I resisted.

The day was a lump, and I was a lump on the lump. It was morning. At some point it became afternoon. Jennifer and Tammy came home but left me to my broken television and tangled thoughts. Then it was dark.

I left the house and walked alone. Though the sun was long down, the air was warm and sticky. Down one block, then another block, past the pretty lawns and wooden fences and hidden cat graves.

At first, I walked aimlessly. Then, to avoid circles, I moved in one general direction. Finally I headed for Harold's house, three quarters of a mile at most. Block, block, block. Corner, corner, corner. No curves where I live. I turned onto Maple Street, breaking into a jog, then a run. I saw my entire life and I wanted none of it. None of it. I spotted his yellow house. The light on the front porch was on, but the windows were dark. It was late, but I had to knock, had to be invited in and asked to sit down and rest. I wanted that. I knocked. Nothing. I knocked again, a little louder. Nothing. Slamming fists. Nothing. I waited, still expecting to see some light from deep inside the house switch on and hear shuffling feet. Nothing. I had run to heaven's gate and the Savior wasn't home.

My legs weak as water, I walked from the door and down the front path. I heard a click and turned. Harold stood in the doorway wearing a sweatshirt and a pair of stained blue jeans.

"It was unlocked," he said and walked back inside leaving the door open.

Blue Harold

The house was warm, the air stale.

"No AC. Too much of a distraction." He walked in front of me slowly, listlessly.

Besides a lamp and some books scattered on the floor, the house was empty.

"Gave everything to the Baptists. Distraction." He scratched his head and walked though the living room. The white walls had slightly whiter rectangular spaces where framed prints no longer hung. The built-in shelves in the living room held nothing but a half-filled glass of water.

When I was five, my family moved from the suburbs of Chicago to Dallas. While clinging to my mother's leg, I watched men in blue jumpsuits strip the walls and lug our belongings away. I discovered my home was simply a house posing as a home. I ran from room to room, spying as the men dismantled all the details. We spent our last night in an empty house, lying awake in the blank space.

Besides a fridge, a stove, and a few glasses, Harold's kitchen was also empty. He poured me a glass of water and turned to me. His face looked yellow and tired. As he handed me a glass, a fear swelled up in my stomach. Who was this man? What was I doing in his house in the middle of the night with questions like, *What do I want? Why am I here?* These questions don't have answers, at least none that satisfy. Like a poison ivy rash, the more you scratch the worse the itch.

"Harold, I—"

"What do you think *Son of God* means, Blake?" he asked, rubbing his face and leaning against his kitchen counter. "*Son-of-God.* The words are too vague. Right now I'm working on *Son.* Then I'll move on to *of.* I doubt I'll even try *God.*"

"What have you got for *Son?*"

"Shared DNA, maybe. Or adoption. A natural contract demanding care. Maybe God has parental instincts. Sons are heirs. Or burdens. Hell, hamsters eat their sons. What good is being a son?" He flinched and pressed his fists to his head.

"You okay?"

"Headaches," he nodded. "Get me sometimes."

"Have you seen a doctor?"

"No. A doctor might make them stop." He lifted himself up to sit on the countertop. "Why are you here?"

"Not sure. Maybe to talk," I said. "I'm not very happy."

He nodded. "There was a boy in my hometown who couldn't feel pain. For a buck, he'd let you punch his face as hard as you want. He wouldn't feel a thing."

"Must be nice."

"He was a slow kid. Didn't talk much. One summer he stepped on a nail. He didn't even know he'd done it. The foot got infected. They had to take it off." He breathed in through his nose. "That's you, Blake."

"What? I'm numb?"

"You want to be," he said. "Can't blame you. I'd hate to feel your life."

No one ever talks about this side of Harold—when his words were cruel and his eyes looked dead. The way they tell it he was always sure, always happy, whistling wisdom to every open ear. That wasn't him. If it had been, I never would have followed.

"Listen, Blake. I'll be gone for a while. I need to think through some things."

Head Shakes and Shrugs

I slouched home. My wife was awake, wiping down a clean kitchen counter with nervous swipes. She looked up as I crept through the back door. I knew the look, the question in her eyes.

"I went for a jog."

"In your slacks?" she asked.

"Spontaneous jog."

"There's a message on the voice mail from the police." She sighed. "They found a drowned dog on Shepherds Drive with our tags."

I puckered my lips and nodded.

"What's going on, Blake?" she asked.

The air conditioning was chilling the sweat off my body and I shivered as I tried to shrug.

"Is something wrong at work?"

I shook my head.

"Is it us? Is it that?"

I shook my head again. I knew it was taking everything in her to ask these questions. Even though I could see the strain in her face, I couldn't say anything, couldn't find any words of comfort. Just head shakes and shrugs.

Seeing her there, red-eyed and cheeks sucked in, I knew there must be as much doubt and life in her as there was in me. But we never showed each other anything. I didn't know how to say anything.

I confess now: I should have loved her more. I remember loving her. She was twenty when we first met. I was twenty-two. I remember her large eyes, brown skin, and a laugh full of hiccups. She smelled like the inside of a snapped branch. We met in the fall and I was in love by the spring. I remember the first night we made love, in her college apartment, muffling moans so her roommate wouldn't hear. Jennifer would bite her pillow. That was wonderful.

Eventually we got our own place. A cheap apartment with skin-thin walls. We still muffled ourselves. No pillow-biting, just quiet. We got married. Still quiet. Hardly a noise. There had been this passion, which we'd bridled for the sake of the roommate or the neighbors. But when we were alone and let go of the reins, the passion whinnied and laid down. Nothing. We bought a big oak bed. Two sides, two tables, two lamps, two novels. Eyes on the page until it was time to close them.

I had a few affairs. One timers, at conferences, once at an office Christmas party. I wanted that old feeling. I wanted the lie that danger tells, the lie that there is more. The lie saying you would scream if you could. But then you can scream and you don't.

You know the best sex Jennifer and I had after we got married? Her mother's house. There in my wife's old room with posters of unicorns and her mother asleep twenty yards away.

Love should be dangerous. There should be a fear of losing control. And a fear of losing the other. Scared to death you'll lose them. Scared to death you'll have to keep them. Scared of the change waiting to drag you down.

That night in the kitchen we stood in silence for a solid minute. Sixty seconds of waiting. No danger was left between us. All I could do was shake my head. All she could do was stare.

"Do you want to, maybe, check in?" she finally said.

For a second—less than that—a hot pressure pulsed behind my eyes, then tears. They came fast, my head leaking like a punctured water balloon.

Jennifer was near, her face a kind blur. She hushed me, took my hand, led me up the stairs, and removed my shoes and clothes. All the while, my tears fell. She crawled in bed beside me, wrapping her arm around my shuddering shoulders. "Hush now," she whispered. "Sleep now."

An Introduction to Haroldism
First Baptism

Over the years, the Haroldian church has developed two annual baptisms. First Baptism is traditionally practiced on the second Sunday of September. It was on this day, many believe, Harold baptized himself in the cold waters of the Frio River in West Texas. Believers reenact the sacrament, baptizing themselves in any body of water available. Though some choose to share this rite with family, it is widely considered a private experience.

Stones Throw (see entry on Second Baptism) is celebrated towards the end of the nine-month liturgical cycle on April 18. For this rite, the presence of others is essential. These two poles of the calendar highlight the Haroldian ideal that both our individuality and our need of community must be embraced and honored. As Harold once said, "We are utterly alone and unavoidably connected. That's who we are."

Mrs. Saint Peter

Today in the basement I read the last page of a half dozen novels I won't have time to read. Today I made faces at a Pastel looking at me from the window in the door. Today I tried to breathe the way Beddy taught me. Today I used the watercolors to paint a portrait of the wife of Saint Peter.

I've never read one word about her, never seen a picture. I know she existed. Jesus heals Peter's mother-in-law, but we never meet a wife. No gospel mentions her. Maybe she had died before Peter met Jesus. Maybe she left him. Maybe she was never around.

I paint her looking away. Streaks of brown, yellow background, streaks and streaks. I wish she'd come visit, drip down through the sprinkler and watch me paint. I'd stand back and let her see my work in progress. She would smile. She would be grateful.

Today I slipped my dinner knife under my mattress. Peter did not seem to notice. An hour later he came back in and asked if I'd seen a "utensil." I shook my head and continued my writing. After he left, I retrieved the knife and examined it. More of a butter knife. I tried attacking my pillow and made only dents. I should have stolen a fork.

Figwood

I wanted to forget about Harold, about my weekend misadventures, about all the questions scavenging around my brain like raccoons in a trashcan. My family helped. Outside of a few side comments and a few concerned looks, my wife never mentioned my shenanigans again. My daughter was no more angry than before.

My greatest ally in forgetting Harold was our town of Figwood, a suburban paradise designed to gloss over any embarrassing flirtations with a spiritual crisis. Figwood, like a mother, cradled and calmed me. "Hey, don't get all excited," she whispered. "Here's the sports page. Don't you need an oil change? Want to learn to golf this weekend?"

Figwood took its name from the fruit that had been its first major industry. In the late 1800s there hadn't been anything in the area but some mosquito-infested woods and several narrow creeks with a tendency to flood. But after the Civil War, a number of former soldiers found riches in the fig. There were fig fields as far as the eye could see. Then the fig industry was replaced with the oil industry and then the technological industry. The figs are long gone and so are the oil and technology. These days, three decades after I left, Figwood's major industry is Harold. It is second only to Austin for holy spots on the Haroldian map. It is a town of hostels, museums, and houses of prayer.

Tammy was five when we first moved to Figwood. We had a house built, choosing from four different floor plans, my wife choosing from four shades of kitchen tiles. We lived less than a mile from the middle school and high school where my daughter would choose from four sports.

Everything was easy.

It was simple to go back to selling computers, paying bills, mowing the lawn. I planned a vacation with my wife and lectured my daughter about her grades. The television still didn't work. I even bought a new one. But that one didn't work either. No problem. My life had cracked, but it would go on. Nothing had to change, I was sure. But Harold wasn't done with me yet.

The Haunted World

On a humid day in early October, I stepped from Promit Computers for lunch and came face-to-face with a smiling Harold. "Good to see you, Blake," he said.

He looked healthier than he had when I last saw him almost four weeks before. He even had a tan. Somehow he had grown sterner than I had remembered him. More solid. And if I hadn't known better, I would say he was taller. His hair was longer too, just a bit. "Letting it grow out?"

He chuckled and patted his head. "I've had a haircut every two weeks for my entire life. I don't want to cut it ever again."

"So where have you been?"

"I went west, traveled around, worked through some things."

"Well, welcome home, I guess." I could hear anger in my voice. It surprised me. "See you around the neighborhood."

"I moved out. The house was too big. I'm living at Autumn Winds now."

"The nursing home?"

"I volunteer a few hours and they give me a room." He smiled as if this was the most natural of living arrangements. "I'm visiting a friend who works near here. Want to join me?"

I hesitated. But not for long.

We walked for half an hour past the faceless office buildings of the Skyline district and on to neighborhoods I'd been warned were too dangerous to even drive through. Storefronts busy with customers, music playing from open windows, fenced in playgrounds with children. The children surprised me most of all. I had never imagined children living in the city. I suppose I never imagined anyone living in the city. The city was a place to work. You lived somewhere else. You had children somewhere else. But there they were, children playing dodgeball a mile from my cubicle.

Harold led me into a small used CD store just east of downtown. It was long and narrow and, at half-past noon, nearly empty. Behind a counter covered with band stickers was a tall black man no older than twenty-five.

"Hello, Steven," Harold said.

"Harold, hey," Steven replied, and I could tell from his undirected gaze that Steven was blind.

"I brought a friend. Blake."

"Good to know you," he said with a nod. "So Harold, you want to play some, or you shopping?"

"Let's play. What do you want?"

"Let's go for maroon."

"Maroon? That might be tough." Harold went flipping through the shelves of CDs. I followed behind him.

"There you go. Thelonious Monk, *Monk's Dream*," he said, handing Steven a CD.

"Really," Steven said with a grin. He gracefully removed the CD from its case and placed it in the stereo. Out poured jazz piano.

"So, that's maroon," Steven said, nodding to the music.

"That's my guess. A little richer than bebop red."

"And there's something sad in it, huh?"

"Yeah, maroon is a little sad. Wagner has some maroon."

That was the game. Music for color. Blue was early Miles Davis. Yellow was the Monkees, but so was Vivaldi. Green was violins. "Smooth but with an edge," Steven said.

He asked if the store was empty and closed up for lunch. "Unless you want to buy anything first?"

Harold looked at me. I shrugged. But Harold didn't look away.

"Okay," I said. "I'll take the one you're playing. Monk."

I raised my eyebrows for Harold, miming the question, "Satisfied?" He smiled.

We walked a couple of blocks to a pizza place, Steven talking the whole time about a girl who came into the store that morning.

"Man, her smell. She smelled like ice cream. She's been by three or four times, and I just can't get up the nerve to ask her name. Ice cream is the sweetest smell, you know, 'cause it makes you think about the taste and two senses get all wrapped up in each other."

We squeezed into a booth with our slices, and Harold asked Steven if he'd always been blind.

"Yeah, I was born blind, but I didn't know it until I was six."

"You didn't know?" I asked.

"No one told me. My grandmother, she raised me, she didn't want me to know. She thought it would make me feel inferior, so she never mentioned anything about sight. Never talked about the way things looked or what pictures were. She just cut those kind of words out of her vocabulary. I was just a kid so I didn't know any better. I thought hearing, smelling, touching, and tasting were all there was."

"What happened?"

"My cousin Nancy stayed with us while her mom was in the hospital. She kept letting things slide like, 'Look at the brown puppy' or 'They painted stripes on the wall.' When I asked my grandmother, she told me it was just new words for old ideas. 'Look' meant touch and 'brown' meant furry. Then she would take my cousin aside and give her a spanking. I remember one time my cousin tried to show me a mirror. I didn't get it at all. 'You see yourself in it,' she said. I touched it and it felt smooth and cold. I just thought my cousin was crazy."

"When did you figure it out?" I asked.

"A couple of things really got me. Like the day she and I were playing in the hallway of our apartment building, and Grandma's sister came out of the elevator. My cousin told me, 'Gracey's coming.' I could hear footsteps from way down the hall, but I couldn't smell Gracey or hear her voice or anything. I just thought my cousin was teasing. Then, after a bit, Gracey was there picking me up and kissing me on the cheek. It was like my cousin knew some kind of magic." Steven stopped and took a quick bite of pizza.

"Then a few days before I turned seven, we were sitting by the window and she said, 'Look at the sunset. It looks like the sky's on fire.' I heard my grandma grab her and whisper some harsh words as she pulled her away. I stood up and walked to the window. It was open. I remember trying to listen for crackling in the sky, you know, like a fire crackles. And I remember trying to feel the heat coming down. The sky was up, I knew that much. And then it got me." Steven shook his head. "I knew something was out there that I didn't know. It came up on me. I couldn't name it or even think it, but there was this whole other thing or world that I didn't know anything about—but my cousin did. A wind blew past, and it scared me so much I fell back and hit the ground."

"It scared you?" I asked.

"Shit, yeah. My grandma picked me up and cradled me saying, 'It's okay. Nancy was teasing. It's okay.' And she started to cry. But, man, I knew. And my grandma's crying made me even more scared."

"What did you do?"

"For a while I did nothing. I was just scared all the time. I didn't want to leave the apartment. I hated being alone. It was like the whole world was haunted. But I grew up and went to school and now I'm here."

"Still scared?" Harold asked.

"Yeah, sometimes," Steven said. "Sometimes in a good way. Music helps."

"Would you ever want to see?" Harold asked.

"I think about that sometimes. How can you want something you can't understand? But, yeah, I'd like to be able to see. I'd like to know what a girl that smells like ice cream looks like."

Harold's Sanity

Harold joined me for lunch the next day and the day after that. I mentioned this to Jennifer. This started her knuckle rubbing.

"He's crazy."

I didn't argue.

"He's probably dangerous."

Again, no argument. I just shrugged.

Some theologian said that Jesus was either a liar, a lunatic, or the Lord. He had to be one of the three, and if the evidence didn't point to liar or lunatic then an honest thinker must accept Jesus as Lord. The same logic has been used to discuss Harold. Liar, lunatic, or lord. But I knew Harold and I'm not sure that the three are mutually exclusive.

"Don't give him any money, Blake."

Irma, or How My Wife Lost Her Housekeeper

Irma cleaned our home twice a week. Irma was black. Irma hated me. She was older, skin like shoe leather and eyes filled with weary resolve. I didn't talk to her much. Jennifer wrote her checks, gave her instructions. She usually came and went while I was at work. But I had started to dread the office, the soft feel of my cubicle chair, the smell of the weaved flooring. I got into the habit of taking sick days, sitting at home doing nothing but listening to the Thelonious Monk CD, and lifting my feet so Irma could vacuum underneath them.

Harold was walking. Everyday, hours on end, he hiked through the suburbs. Occasionally I joined him, but often he was alone. One afternoon I saw him strolling along the sidewalk in front of my house. I opened the front door and called his name. As he turned and waved, Irma pushed by me and ran out to the sidewalk yelling, "I know you! I know you!"

She and Harold stood talking for a few minutes, both laughing, sometimes glancing back at me. Then they hugged, and he went on his way.

Irma returned to the house, walked right by me into my little wet bar and poured herself a straight whiskey. I just stared. It was so strange that to object seemed absurd.

"I'm not cleaning your house anymore," she said and fell back on one of the leather armchairs in our living room.

"Okay," I said.

"So, you know that man?"

I nodded. She nodded and sipped.

"And you know him?" I asked.

"Oh yeah. But I didn't know his name till just now," she said. I sat on the edge of the couch. She took another sip and looked up at me. "You know, Mr. Waterson, I hate cleaning rich people's houses."

"I'm not rich," I said.

"Have you seen where I live?"

"No."

"You're rich." She finished her drink, gathered her chemicals and soap, and left. Later, I asked Harold what he and Irma had talked about.

"None of your concern, Blake."

An Introduction to Haroldism
Irma Bragston

Each of Harold's original followers brought essential elements to the burgeoning movement. Irma Bragston was a devout Southern Baptist who melded her more traditional faith with Harold's teachings. She, more than any of Harold's closest followers, related his teachings using Christian terminology and imagery. Many credit her as being a bridge between conservative Christianity and the new faith.

Her dedication to the Southern Baptist church never faltered. Even when the denomination declared Haroldism heretical, Irma Bragston held strong, courageously speaking her convictions. She and her daughter were publicly persecuted and harshly criticized by many church leaders.

The efforts backfired. Parishioners responded by rallying behind the Bragstons, some turning to Haroldism for the first time. Many Church historians mark this persecution as the beginning of the end of any major Southern Baptist influence in America.

Most Treasured Memory

My wife blamed me for the loss of Irma.

"But I didn't do *anything*."

"Oh, I'm sure you didn't."

She disapproved of my sick days, of my walks with Harold, of my spaced-out look. I wanted to explain, or at least try to explain, what was happening. How everything was falling into question. But the sand was so packed down we couldn't get near each other.

We had been happy at one time. I remember the three of us—me, Jennifer, and Tammy—renting films on Friday nights. It was family night. I remember years before, watching Disney's *Beauty and the Beast*, Tammy, only six, falling asleep on the floor, Jennifer resting her head on my lap, dozing as well, me all toasty with gin and tonic, and the Beast full of courage and love. There we were. Cocooned. Happy and safe enough to fall asleep. I had the love of these women. Unquestioning love. Jennifer wrapped her warm arm around my thigh like it was a pillow. I would lift Tammy's little body, carry her to bed, and tuck her in. Later my wife and I would sleep close enough to smell nothing but each other. This is my most treasured memory. Life was fine. I had it. I lost it.

Questions

Question I asked Harold:

"Does life have meaning?"

Harold's answer:

"What would you tell your daughter?"

No Sky at All

No windows to the outside in this basement. The one in the door shows nothing but a short hallway. No sky. I know it's night. I can tell it's dark outside, though I've got every light turned on inside. I can smell it.

I dab my watercolors. Beddy drips through the air vent and sits on my cot. Beddy was Harold's finest disciple. Harold's favorite, I think. I tell Beddy I'm writing a confession. I tell him I'm remembering things. He smiles and brushes back his bangs. I tell him I'm dying and he nods.

I tell him I remember walking. Weeks of walking. I remember places where we could stop for a Slurpee or a Big Mac every mile. And other places that few roads led to. And still further out. One night we slept in an abandoned house. Flakes of paint and rotting floors. Dusk sucked all the light out of the sky. Dark night, days from anywhere. I had lost the world.

I remember too, Beddy says.

I go back to painting. He stays. He'll stay most of the night, watching me paint, whistling every so often.

Sight

When we next visited the CD store, Steven was sitting on a stool behind the counter.

"Hey, Steven," Harold said as we walked in. Steven looked at us. He looked directly at us.

"Harold?" he asked. He raised his chin and peered at us from the bottom of his eyes. It made his face look anxious, restless.

"Yeah, it's me."

"Did you do this?"

"Do what?"

"Just tell me."

"What's happened, Steven?" Harold asked.

"If you did this," he stood from his stool and started to walk around the counter, but he slammed into it, knocking down a stack of CDs. "Shit! I can't even walk." Steven knelt down and began collecting the fallen CDs. Harold joined him.

"Steven, can you see?" I asked.

"I don't know. There's all this stuff pouring in—I guess through my eyes 'cause I can close them. And I do. I close them a lot."

"Why close them? If you can see, I mean—"

"Are you Blake?" he looked up at me and blinked his eyes. I nodded, but he still looked without any trace of understanding.

"Yeah, I'm Blake," I said.

"You don't get it." He picked up a CD. "I know this is a CD. I can feel it with my hands, I can even read the Braille title, but," he dropped it back on the ground and pointed at it, "I couldn't tell you what that is. I couldn't even tell you its shape."

"But you can see. You'll get the other stuff."

"And then there's this. He stood up and felt around on the counter. His fingers reached a CD and he lifted it. "This is maroon, right?"

"Yes," I said.

"But it isn't Monk. I mean the color, it's nothing like music. So I keep thinking the color's wrong. It was better as music. I'm confused as shit and my head hurts." His voice cracked.

"Give it some time, Steven. It's all new," Harold said, placing a hand on Steven's back. Steven spun around.

"Did you do this?"

Harold shrugged. "I don't control these things," he said.

"You don't?" I asked.

"I don't. Really. They just happen around me."

"Harold, I can't even recognize myself. I look in a mirror and . . ." He swallowed whatever he was going to say. "It's just so different. It's nothing like I thought it was. And it hurts."

"Hold on, Steven," Harold said.

"My grandmother was right. It was better not to know." Then Steven asked us to leave.

Waves

Outside the sky was sick cloud white. The air stunk of trapped car fumes and cement. We didn't talk as we made our way back toward the office. I wanted to ask Harold about Steven, about not controlling the miracles, about my television. But he was thinking. I looked at him out of the corner of my eye. His head was bent down, puzzled. Maybe it was the crow's feet coming from his squinting eyes or his stooped posture—he looked old and hurt.

He asked me, "Do you think it's better not to see?"

"I don't know," I said.

"Would you drive me to Galveston?"

"Now? It's an hour away."

"There's something I want to show you."

We drove east from the city, passing the suburbs and the exit for Figwood and then Clear Lake, where the astronauts used to live. Past refineries with smoke and burning torches, and then salty marshes and the arched bridge that lands on the island of Galveston. Within an hour we were looking at the brown waters of the Gulf of Mexico.

Harold and I sat on the sea wall looking out and counting seagulls and oil wells. It was windy, a little cold. Above the rhythmic white noise of the surf were the sporadic screams of seagulls. The beach was empty of people. Just sand, patches of tar, and trash blown along by the fish-tainted breeze.

"God is ancient and ever new," Harold said. "God is the constant and the revolution. God gives and then gives again. Watch the waves, Blake."

And I did. Each one new, pushing in, and before it even had a chance to fall completely away another wave pushing over.

"But it's all the same water," Harold said. "The wave is just a wave. It's the ocean that shapes the sand, not the wave." Then he turned to me. "Never think the wave you ride is more or less than the thousands before or the thousands after."

I watched the muddy water and said nothing. I was afraid if I spoke Harold would see that I didn't understand. Harold pressed the heels of his palms against his temples.

"Headache again?"

"Migraine. Adds light to things," he said. "Starts in the corner of my eyesight, a mirrored hole. After an hour it covers everything I see. Right now, I can't make out half your face."

"Harold, you should see someone about that."

He shook his head. "It's the crack that lets the colors in."

We sat still for a few minutes, the waves pulsing against the sand.

"I want you to quit your job," he said after a few minutes.

I laughed.

"It's not your vocation, Blake."

I asked what my vocation was.

"I don't know," he said. He sounded surprised I would even ask.

"You don't know? What kind of messiah are you?"

"One who doesn't know," he said with a dry laugh.

Something was so sad about that day. Something in those pointless waves he wanted me to watch. All the same water. Clawing at sand. Like he said, thousands. Doing nothing but moving sand. Shaping and scraping and gone again.

"What are you going to do, Harold?" I asked.

"I think I'll walk to Austin."

"That's two hundred miles away. You're going to *walk* there?"

"Yep," he said. "Strange thing to do."

Surprise

That night, at the dinner table, I told Jennifer and Tammy that I had written a letter of resignation.

"You're quitting?" Tammy asked through a mouthful of food.

"Is this because of Harold?"

"This is a good thing," I said. I tried to explain about vocation and waves, but it came out mumbled and unconvincing. "I want us to be more alive. Happier."

"Are you going to get another job?" Tammy asked.

"Sure, I guess. Eventually."

"So, how do we eat until then, Blake?" Jennifer was rubbing her knuckles red. "How does Tammy go to college?"

"We have some savings and if we sell the house and move—"

"Sell the house!" My wife stood up. "This house? I decorated this house. Where else would we live?"

"We could get an apartment or something. You know, Harold gave—"

"Tammy," my wife said. "Please excuse us, will you?"

"Are you kidding me?" Tammy said. My wife gripped the table's edge and stared down. Tammy sighed, pushed back her chair with a screech, and stomped upstairs.

Jennifer waited until Tammy was out of earshot then addressed me with a sternness that I'd never known from her. "Blake, if you're going to have a midlife crisis, just buy a convertible for God's sake."

"This is not just a phase. I want to rethink things."

"Harold is sick. He is dangerous and needs psychiatric help."

"But he makes some good points," I said.

"Have you given him any money? Have you?"

"No."

She folded her arms and stared at me. She nodded her head. A decision had been made. She left the room.

I sat at the table and watched our leftover food grow cold. I sat there for an hour. The food didn't move. I tried to see if the rotting had begun. I knew it must have, but I couldn't tell.

Then I went to bed.

The lights were out. I undressed and crawled under the sheets. She was still, but I knew she was awake. I thought to touch her, but something in her quietness told me to keep a distance. So I lay and watched the back of her head. I wasn't close enough to smell her hair, but I could remember the scent. The color had faded, but not the smell. A clean, alive, snapped branch smell. I remembered years before deciding it was my favorite smell in the world.

"I'm leaving you, Blake," she said in a whisper so gentle that she never lost her stillness. "It's not for me. I can take it. It's for Tammy. Tomorrow, okay. I want you to be gone tomorrow."

Want a shock? I was surprised.

Want another? I was heartbroken.

But I did not argue. Instead I went downstairs for a drink. No shock there.

I turned off every light and fixed myself a gin and tonic in the dark. Besides the hum of the refrigerator and the tapping of ice in my glass, the house was silent. It was so quiet I could hear the wind outside. Jennifer wanted me to leave. I had things to think about, but I had no intention of thinking. Another drink. This time with a little less tonic and a little more gin.

In the dark, the house was unfamiliar and full of shadows. A car passed and all the shadows did a dance across the living room. I wanted them to dance more, so I had another drink, and another. I ran out of tonic but that was all right with me. Another drink. Soon the shadows were dancing whenever I moved my head.

Now, all these years later, the same shadows are still with me. Around me and in me. No longer dancing. Crawling. Patches of dark and patches of darker dark asking me why I didn't love her more. Asking why I didn't go upstairs and promise to be a better man, or at least let her know I didn't want to go. Shadows telling me that there is something essential I'm not seeing. Something deep below my marriage, my child, my Harold, my life. Below words. Something that I hunger for with all my desires and mistakes. A buried thing I need, which promises only that it will never be found. Now, as then, as always.

This night in the basement, I watch those shadows. Eyes open.

That night in my living room, I closed my eyes. All the shadows slinked into my head and slid down into my stomach. They spun around inside me, dancing too quickly. On instinct, I got up, stumbled into the bathroom, and knelt with my hands pressed against the commode. The shadows were trying to climb out of my stomach, up my throat, and out of my mouth. That familiar acidic spit paving the way. But I wasn't going to let them out this time. The shadows were staying. I swallowed and clenched my teeth.

"You're not going anywhere," I said and passed out on the toilet seat.

Moving Out

I woke up in the bathroom with my brain a water balloon two sizes too large for my skull. Jennifer and Tammy had left for the day. A note from Jennifer explained that I should be gone by evening. I wrote a reply on the back of the note saying that she was the one leaving me, why should I move? And, hey, who sold half-a-fucking-million computers to buy this house that I'm now being told to leave? Then I shoved the note down the disposal.

The house felt empty. Everything was still there but it was empty. I went through each room looking, touching things, wondering why they didn't anchor me down. I found myself sitting in Tammy's room, on her bed, staring at posters of rock bands and polar bears. Clothes were everywhere and magazines scattered the floor. Tammy's plastic gumball machine sat on her dresser. It only had three gumballs left. Soon they'd be gone. What then? What would she do?

I drove to the Autumn Winds nursing home where Harold had moved. I parked the car and sat. I was sweating. Click goes the key. Quiet goes the engine. All the world is a window away.

Terry Williamson was walking out of Autumn Winds. I had not talked to him since the night Pickles died and Harold ruined our dinner party. He didn't see me. He put on his designer sunglasses and brushed back his red curls. He climbed into a forest green SUV and drove away. I waited till he was gone and headed for the building.

I hated the place as soon as I stepped inside. It was relatively new, but so cheaply built that after two decades it was already decrepit. Plastered lobby walls growing yellow and ceilings stained with brown water. The lower half of the lobby walls were covered with childish drawings. I looked around for Harold but saw nothing but brittle, ashy men and women pointing out their paintings while their middle-aged children stood beside them nodding. "That's a very nice painting, Mom. It's very pretty."

A tall desk stood in the center of the room, and a woman in a nurse's uniform was sitting behind it.

"Are you here for the residents' art show?" she asked.

"No, I'm looking for Harold Peeks."

She told me she'd get him and handed me a plastic badge which read "VISITOR." I was glad to have it. Glad to have a label that told everyone and myself that I did not belong here. I randomly stared at the paintings while waiting. Most were done with watercolors. Watercolors depress me. So thin, so pale, so weak, so faded, as if maybe it had once been real paint, once had real colors, but not anymore. Too similar to the gray-skinned residents.

"How do you like it?" said a small voice beside me. The voice belonged to a short, wrinkled woman with a big smile.

"It's very nice," I said, realizing I had been staring at a painting of what I can only assume was supposed to be a horse. That or a large dog wearing a saddle.

"I'm the artist," she said, beaming.

"You obviously have a lot of talent." I looked around for an escape.

"Thank you," she said. "Would you like to see my papier-mâché egg?"

"No, no. I don't like eggs." Just then I saw Harold waving at me from down the hall.

"Oh," said the woman. "You're one of his."

"No," I said. "I am not." And I walked down the hall.

I passed room after room with open doors. Each had a narrow bed with a yellow or blue blanket and a small television. Each smelled of vinegar and damp air. Some rooms were occupied with thin bodies lying down or sitting in straight-backed chairs. I caught snippets of sitcoms and game shows as I walked by. Halfway down the hall on the right side was a large open area filled with a dozen slow moving figures in bathrobes and pajamas. Another television blared commercials.

When I was a boy, my father, the good doctor, used to take me with him as he did his rounds at a local nursing home. He told me a young face would cheer them up. So we'd go and I'd stick by his side, avoiding their reaching hands. But then he'd disappear into a room and leave me for them. They'd grab me, turning me towards them and staring with watery eyes. Back then I thought they were trying to steal my youth, trying to suck life out of me with their eyes. As I grew up I realized what a silly idea that is, but now that I'm old I think I was right the first time. I fear old people. I fear old. Old, mold, moldy . . . skin that doesn't fit anymore, purple bruises, leaking memories and mucus and urine.

Harold was wearing pale blue scrubs—the cheap kind, like the girl who cleans your teeth. They were too small for him. In his hand he had a large sugar cookie with the word *ART* spelled out in pink icing

"Was Terry Williamson here to see you?" I asked Harold once I got inside.

"Yes."

"What did he want?"

"That's none of your concern, Blake," he said. "Want a cookie?"

I sat down on the room's one chair. "My wife is leaving me."

He sat on the bed and bit his cookie, right through the *A*.

"Because of me?" he asked.

"Partially."

"I'm sorry," he said and rubbed his eyes. "I wish I could give you some peace."

I nodded.

"But I've come to shatter things." He took another bite. "Have you quit your job yet?"

"No."

"Are you going to?"

"I'm not sure."

"Is it worth the hours?"

"What would I do otherwise?"

"That's not the question."

I drove to Promit Computers and turned in my letter of resignation. Then I went back to Autumn Winds and fell asleep on Harold's floor.

Dreaming of Now

That night, sleeping on a nursing home floor, I dreamt of now. Of an old man sitting in a basement, in front of a Van Gogh painting. *Cypresses*. Inky black and green over blue. Of course, it's just a print. You can't touch the texture of the paint strokes. The print is a hint. The room is a tomb.

I'm as restless today as I was then. Like there's something to do, but I can't quite get it done. Deeper down, if I let all that restlessness blow away, I see the real joke: nothing ever gets done. Nothing real. You think it does, but it's all just bill paying and pleasure having and time killing. Nothing really happens.

Nothing happens and time is running out. I know I'm dying. It feels lonely. I think it's what's made me lonely my whole life. Not death as an end, but death as an always. It's like dancing on an iced pond, that cold water always just an inch below you. You keep your feet moving so you won't crack through. But the cold still makes you shiver. Always there. And if you stop dancing, just for a second, that cold air creeps up your legs, soaks in. Cold just below. Death right there. Trying to tell me it's already in my veins.

God, you hear this? You hear what the cold is telling me? What nature keeps whispering? How much this all hurts? Do you hear this, you mute? I put my ear to your chest and listen for a heartbeat. I can't hear a heartbeat.

Please don't leave me like this. I'm undone.

Questions

Question I asked Harold:

"Is there an afterlife?"

Harold's answer:

"If there is, I bet you'll spend it the same way you're spending this moment."

Following

On my second night at Autumn Winds, I met Shael. Young, late twenties, maybe thirty. Dark eyes, dark hair. Her cheeks curving in on her face like shallow valleys. Her mouth, somber and small. She walked into Harold's tiny room smelling of cigarette smoke. She seemed surprised, disappointed surprised, to see Harold was not alone. She had brought him a rose with a broken stem, which she handed over with no smile, as if it were something she had just picked up from the floor. He grinned and pinned the rose to his blue scrubs.

I offered to leave but Harold stopped me. He made a few calls and a little makeshift party started to form. Irma came, scrunching her face at me, but cordial enough. Gilbert Forncrammer, bald-headed and frantic, pushed through the door.

"Well, goddamn it, Texas is humid," he grunted and sat down on the bed next to Shael. "How can you live here, Harold? Goddamn old people stinking up the place."

"You're not so fresh out of the box yourself, Gilbert," Harold said from his seat on the floor.

"I'm seventy-eight. That's not synonymous with old."

The next hour was an exchange of stories. I sat in the corner while the others talked. Shael described her childhood summers in Colorado.

"It was cold at night and hot during the day. And everything smelled of pine," she said. She described the stream she and her brother would swim in. "The kind of cold that hurts, but we kept swimming, every day of the summer."

Irma told us about falling in a frozen creek when she was a child. Gilbert stood up and showed us how he used to run in place to keep warm when he worked as a night watchman. Within the laughing and talking was a strange excitement. It was as if each one of them had carried in an armful of energy and piled it in the center of the room. Even from my spot on the edge of the group, against the wall and close to the door, I could feel that energy spiraling.

Sometime after eleven a nurse knocked on the door and asked if we'd quiet down. "And you," she looked directly at Gilbert. "You should be in your bed."

"I don't live here," he protested, but she had already gone. "Well, hell."

Harold jumped up and announced that we were going out and headed for the door. No time for discussion. It was follow or not follow.

After the stale air of the small room, the outside breeze was a welcome breath. The street was quiet and we went stomping into the silence, the puddles splashing beneath us. And me, smiling and following in spite of myself. "Oh, my, my," Irma kept saying. Harold talked to us over his shoulder. "Once you find life, give it away. Give it in large and small portions to whoever's around. You'll find more."

The only bar in sight, maybe the only bar in Figwood, was a few blocks distance, sharing a strip mall with a video store and a hot wings delivery.

Shael lit a cigarette as we tumbled in. Harold leaned into me. "Finding life and being found. That's it. You okay?"

I nodded. He patted my back. The bar was tacky and empty of other customers. An abundance of blue neon bounced off the walls. Near the back, a jukebox belted out an old Bon Jovi song.

Shael and Harold danced, making clumsy circles and laughing. I wondered what Jennifer was doing, wondered if I should call home. I took a seat next to Irma. She tapped her toes and swayed in her seat, careful to keep her back to me. Gilbert had stationed himself at the bar, and I got up and joined him.

"You shouldn't eat peanuts at bars," he said as I sat down. "Fecal matter."

"Excuse me?"

"Men go take a crap, come back to the bar, shove a hand into the dish. Fecal matter." He lifted a fist-full of peanuts and poured it in his mouth.

"So why are you eating them?"

He shrugged. "I like salty things."

I nodded and ordered a drink.

"I think Harold is a crazy bastard," he said. "You?"

I looked over to Harold dancing, sweating dark patches though his scrubs. They were starting to tear under the arms.

"Yeah. He's crazy."

"Good."

We nodded.

"Then why are you here?" I asked.

He put his drink down. "Vegas," he said, letting the word slide out slowly. "I can tell you, if you want."

"Okay."

"But it's a little left of day-to-day, alright?"

I nodded. He took a breath and began.

"Not to brag, but I am very rich." He raised his eyebrows, which made his whole scalp wrinkle. "I own Pagemore Beef and a good part of Rose Shipping and a few banks."

"Wow," I said and meant it. Rich people always impressed me.

"Oh yeah. I'm king of All Shit Mountain. A few weeks ago, I was turning seventy-eight and feeling twenty. Feeling like a goddamned twenty-year-old. So I took a vacation to Vegas with this girl I sometimes run around with." He motioned to the bartender for another round. "We checked in, made love on the balcony, then again in the hot tub, and got something to eat. My girlfriend went shopping and I strolled the casino. You gamble?"

I shook my head.

"Well, a gambler knows you never bet on a whim, nor do you waste time on slots. Slots suck. But what the hell, I had some time, I had some cash. I'm standing at a dollar slot when someone behind me says, 'That machine won't win, but the next one will.' I turn around and there's Harold. Of course, I didn't know him from Adam at the time, so I tell him to back off and I drop the coin. And he says, 'Two roses and a barrel.' The wheels spin and guess what they land on?"

"Two roses and a barrel?"

"Damn right! Then he says again that the next machine will win, so I don't even look at him. I just move over to the next machine and drop in another buck. 'Three shamrocks,' he says. And what do you know, three shamrocks and the machine spits out fifty bucks. So I ask Harold if he's some kind of psychic and he says, 'No. I'm the Son of God.' And I say, 'I don't care if you're the Son of Sam, I like your style.' Then I ask him if he's breaking any laws. And he says no. So I ask him if he likes roulette." Gilbert gulped his drink and licked his lips.

"Hot damn, that was fun. In an hour I'm up ten thousand and laughing my ass off. Around midnight my girlfriend comes looking for me, but I just send her to bed. I mean, hell, what a streak. Harold hadn't missed a call all night. Twenty-three, fourteen, five. He just kept calling them and I kept placing them.

"Then, out of the blue, he turns to me and asks, 'Do you want to win or do you want what's best?' Well, I tell him I want to win, so he gives me the number and I win. Then he asks again, 'Do you want to win or what's best?' Well, I tell him that I think winning is best. And he nods, gives me a number, and I win again. Then he asks, 'Do you want to win or what's best?' And I tell him I think I can figure out what's best and he says, 'You can't even figure out where the ball is going to land. How can you figure out what's best?' I ask him who can and he shrugs. Then I ask him if he's a Mason, 'cause I don't trust Masons and I don't want to be one. You're not a Mason, are you Blake?"

"No," I answered.

"Okay then," Gilbert nodded to himself. "Where was I?"

"Win or best."

"Oh yeah. So I finally give in and say, 'Best.' He says, 'Pick seven.' I call seven and the ball lands on nine. Again he asks the win or best question. I say, 'Best' and he says pick seven again. And I lose again. I look right at Harold and say, 'Best.' 'Seven' and I lose again, but I didn't even see it land. I call seven again, this time all the chips. I lose them all, but I'm still watching Harold. Then I pull out my credit card and tell them to stack it to the limit. Twenty thousand on seven. The dealer gets nervous and has to call an owner, but soon enough the wheel spins and the ball bounces and lands snap-damn on the number eight. I lost it all."

He laughed and bit down on a piece of ice. "Best night of my life," he said. "What about you? What's your story?"

"He broke my television."

"Damn," he shook his head. "Crazy bastard."

I looked back at Harold. He was sitting now. So were the others. The scrubs had torn, exposing a good a chunk of one of his armpits each time he sipped his beer. As I watched, he started tugging at the rip and removed one sleeve completely. But the other he left hanging on. He was laughing and banging his hands on the table as if it were a piano.

"So now I'm here," Gilbert said. "Ready to walk to Austin."

"You're going with him?" I turned back.

"Hell yeah. He asked me to come and I'm going. How about you?"

"I . . . I wasn't invited."

"Well, what's the saying? Many are called. Few are chosen." He got up, patted my back, and went to join the others.

I had thought Harold was going alone. I hadn't wanted to walk to Austin. But now, now that I knew I wasn't invited, wasn't chosen, all I wanted was to go. I headed for the door, suddenly tired.

Outside it was quiet and it had grown colder. Most of Figwood was asleep.

"Leaving, Blake?"

It was Harold. He had taken the detached sleeve and wrapped it around his head.

I was a child asking to hang out with his big brother's gang. "Harold, can I go to Austin?"

He said no. I added please. He still said no. I asked a third time and he said we should go for a walk.

In the made-for-television movie *Harold Be Thy Name*, there is a famous scene of Harold and me walking through Figwood and coming to the edge of the highway. The cars speed past at seventy miles per hour.

"Blake, you must trust me," Harold says. "Follow me." He steps into a blur of traffic and walks unscathed to the far side. No horns honk, no cars swerve. When watching you can't tell if Harold's walking is so well-timed that he misses each car or if he somehow passes through the cars as if they weren't there. Then, from the other side, Harold turns back to me and mouths the words, "Follow me." I hesitate, watching the cars plow by. I reach out a foot and quickly pull it back as a red sports car screams past. The wind from the traffic blows against my face. Past the cars, I see the eyes of Harold. I take a deep breath and step. The cars continue to race, the wind blows, but I walk safely into the river of steel with my eyes locked on Harold. A minivan whips past my face and I yelp. I take my eyes off Harold. I see the cars streaming toward me and I start to panic. Horns start honking and cars start swerving. An eighteen-wheeler is headed right for me.

"Harold, save me!" I yell. And in an instant I am safe with Harold on the far side of the highway.

"Why didn't you trust me?" Harold asks, a hand on my shoulder. I shrug and we walk on.

This never happened. But it made for great TV.

What did happen on that walk was far more dramatic for me. It was a sentence.

"You have to learn what grace is," Harold told me. "You'll need it." He went to stick his hands in his pockets, but scrubs don't have pockets. He just rubbed his legs.

"We start walking in two days," he said.

The Beast Is the Least

Peter lingers. He brings in my meal and often stays until I'm done, sometimes speaking, sometimes pacing the basement with his hands behind his back.

Yesterday he watched me paint a picture of the sky, adding layers of blue—morning clear, midday haze, evening thick.

"You believe in God, don't you?" he asked. I nodded towards my canvas and added some cloud wisps. "Does that give you any peace?"

"Resignation."

"Must be nice," he said.

"Ups and downs," I said.

He helped to hang my *Mrs. Saint Peter* between Gauguin's *The Bathers* and Van Gogh's *Cypresses*.

"Good company," I said. "They were friends, you know. Gauguin and Van Gogh. Almost killed each other, but friends."

"I didn't know."

"I read about it. Friends, but totally different styles of painting. Van Gogh would hunt for images, find the perfect cypress, set up his easel outside and paint what he saw. Gauguin made it all up in his head. Painted inside from memories and what he could imagine. You know what that means?"

Peter shook his head.

"It means that the cypress really existed and the bathers were made up."

"Oh," he said.

"Does it matter? I mean, now, looking at these paintings."

He grunted and turned to leave.

"May I ask you something?" I asked as he reached the stairs. "Why am I being cared for? Why not just turn me in?"

He nodded at a plaque on the wall and walked on.

Take your greatest enemy, the one who stole everything from you, and give him a home. Give him food and care, and you will be giving to God.

Harold Peeks

So there you go. I'm the least of these. I'm the greatest enemy. To love me is to love God. When Peter leaves, I take my paintbrush and walk to the entrance of the bathroom. One of the wall's cinderblocks has a jagged edge. I kneel down and begin sharpening the handle of my paintbrush into a dagger. I'll use it to stab him in the neck. Then I'll run run run.

BOOK II

Packing

"Bring whatever you want," he told me. "But know that you'll have to carry all you bring and you'll lose all you carry."

"So you're saying I should bring nothing?"

"Yeah, but you don't believe me."

I didn't. I went to my home, careful to stop by while my wife and daughter were away, and collected three weeks worth of clothes, shoes, and toiletries. I then went to an REI and bought an aluminum internal framed backpack, a synthetic down sleeping bag, and a yellow and black North Face Teflon jacket—perfect for rain, cold, and wind. I also purchased wool socks, sunblock, and an extra pair of waterproof leather hiking boots. I was set.

"What about money?" I had asked Harold.

He said a hundred would do it. Said we'd pool the money. I nodded and packed my credit card.

The morning we were set to leave, I shoved all my supplies into my new pack. It looked like some extracted tumor leaning against the wall of Harold's room.

"That's too heavy," Harold said.

"I'll manage."

Irma arrived wearing a simple flowered dress and carrying a bag half the size of mine.

"Is that your bag?" she asked, setting hers beside mine. I nodded.

"Well, you won't die of exposure."

Harold laughed and went off to collect some breakfast from the dining room, leaving Irma and me alone.

"I didn't know you were joining us," I said, just an attempt at small talk.

"'Cause I'm a woman or because I'm old?"

"No, I just—"

"I've been on my feet all my life. A little bit longer won't kill me." She sat down on Harold's bed and tightened her shoelaces.

Shael showed up a few minutes later, half nodding at me and giving Irma a long hug. Gilbert walked in almost immediately after, cussing about taxi prices and bad drivers.

"Hot-piping dog crap," he said as he stumbled into my backpack. "Who packed the closet?" I excused myself to help Harold with the food.

Harold and I were balancing bowls of oatmeal when we came upon Terry standing in the hallway, a pack on his back as stuffed as mine. He was wearing sunglasses, a flannel shirt, and the same designer hiking boots I had in my bag.

"I'm taking my vacation days, and Beth is fine with me going," Terry said with a nervous smile.

"Terry, I told you, this walk isn't for you," Harold said.

"But I want to go. I want to follow."

"Go home to your wife."

Terry opened his mouth to argue but stopped. He glanced at me, embarrassed, envious. He nodded to Harold and walked down the hall with his backpack and new boots. Harold watched him go.

"Are you going to send me away as well?" I asked with a light chuckle.

"You should be so lucky," he said. And how I wished he would've smiled when he said it.

First Steps

We began walking on an unseasonably warm November morning. Stepped out from the door of Autumn Winds and headed west. It must have been a laugh for the locals, seeing us march down the street like overage scouts. We skirted a golf course and walked past the middle school, crossed Main Street, and made our way through the older neighborhoods on the east side of town.

After three hours of walking, I realized something horrible. We were only ten minutes from Autumn Winds. That is, ten minutes by car. Three hours and we had hardly left. I never imagined how long a mile really was until that day. You step and step and step and barely move.

On a shady street on the east side, a boy on a dirt bike rode beside us, swerving to keep balanced at such a slow pace.

"Where you guys going?" he asked.

"Austin," I told him.

"Why don't you guys get a car?"

"Because then we'd never have met you," Harold said.

"That's kind of stupid," he said. "I had to slow down to meet you." He sped away on his dirt bike and was out of sight within half a minute.

It took half a day of walking before we left the Figwood city limits. My feet were already hurting, my legs were cramping, and the straps of my bag dug into my shoulders like overzealous bondage gear. What I had packed felt heavier than my body. The world was suddenly large. Distances meant more. Austin was too far away to imagine.

Harold said it was better that we walk, that we see and feel the miles. In America, he said, you can travel a thousand miles and not feel a thing, you can meet a thousand people, live a thousand years, and still not feel a thing. "It's the glory of our nation. The promise. Give us your poor, your troubled . . . they won't feel a thing. It might be over a hundred degrees outside, but we have air conditioning. You won't feel a thing. And if it gets cold, we'll put on the heater. And you won't feel a thing. Yes, we'll execute him, but he won't feel a thing. Yes, you're dying, but we'll make sure you don't feel a thing."

From the start we were learning to feel everything. That's what he wanted. He wanted blisters and tears as much as laughter and food. He sucked up experience. So we walked.

An Introduction to Haroldism
Community Pilgrimage

Walking the Holy Road to Austin is the centerpiece of Haroldian ritual. The Road has no official starting point. In fact, many people begin walking from their own front door. But wherever a group starts, they eventually pass through Figwood, Texas, and from there on to Austin. Every year thousands of pilgrims from all over the world follow a route indicated by three-foot-high stone markers each engraved with a brick-red **H**.

It is common to walk with a group to Austin and to use the time to celebrate community and family. As Harold himself said, "We find God amongst each other." Groups ranging from two to two hundred walk together singing the many songs that have developed honoring the Road. The lyrics capture the joys and struggles of the walk. For example:

We stride, we stride. To Austin, to Austin.
To Austin we roam.
We stride, we stride. To Austin, to Austin.
The home we've never known.

Another example:

And though our hearts are heavy,
Our lives are full of pain,
Soon we'll be in Austin,
And be made whole again.

A series of pilgrim hostels have been established along the Road which charge little or no money for a bed and a shower. These hostels with their communal kitchens and dining rooms epitomize the feeling of family and unity that the Road represents. The hostels were founded and are maintained by the Haroldian Order of Service. These men and women live in monastic communities and dedicate their lives to serving those who seek Harold. Recently a host of private hostels offering more luxurious accommodations have also popped up along the Road.

Though walking is the most common way to travel to Austin, bicycling has become more and more popular. Some also drive or join an organized bus tour. However one travels, the journey to Austin is a joy-filled rite every Haroldian should experience.

Pain

I didn't mention my blisters. Just gritted my teeth and walked. Irma was the first to complain.

"Harold, we've got to stop. I'm hurting."

"What hurts?"

"My knees, my ankles, my everything."

"Don't feed the pain," he said, walking as he talked. "The more you feed the pain, the more it will hound you and the bigger it will grow."

"So what? Ignore anything that hurts?" Gilbert asked.

"Acknowledge it. Be aware of pain, but don't hate it, don't dwell on it, don't feed it." He stopped and sighed. "We'll take a break."

Why Austin?

"Where the flat ends and the hills begin," he told us. "There are rivers under Austin."

"Fine, but really? Why there?" I asked.

"A feeling," he said. "Austin is the place. Everything that is supposed to happen will happen there."

"A feeling? We're walking over two hundred miles for a feeling?"

He stared at me, his eyes squinting. "No one's pointing a gun at you, Blake. You can go home. I'm walking to Austin."

Unpacking

I started unpacking from the start, purposely forgetting my electric razor in a gas station bathroom and leaving a couple of sweaters at a campsite. It wasn't generosity. I just wanted a lighter load.

I did it all on the sly, not letting the others know how right they had been about the size of my pack.

Losing my extra pair of hiking boots gave me trouble. On our fourth night out, we slept in a park next to picnic tables. Just before we set off that morning, I took the boots from my backpack and, while no one was looking, left them on one of the tables.

"Blake," Gilbert tapped my shoulder as we started walking. "Aren't those your shoes back there?"

"Oh yeah. Thanks." And I ran back to retrieve them. I didn't put them in my bag. I tied the laces together, draped them around my neck, and waited for a chance to lose them along the way.

That day we walked through a subdivision, Wooded Estates or Oak Terrace or something. A carefully crafted collection of boxes. Great for walking—well-kept sidewalks, trees for shade, and low traffic. You could stroll all day long, but leaving was nearly impossible. There was no direct route out. The roads looped back into themselves, cut into each other, or just ended in cul-de-sacs. It took us an hour to discover the subdivision's one exit was the same road we had used to enter. All that walking and we had gotten nowhere.

At the exit/entrance, the sidewalks ended, the glossy grass stopped growing, and not a house or a tree was to be seen. So we walked single file on the rocky shoulder of a farm road. If I had been driving, I would have described it as a slow country road with mild traffic. While walking, it was a narrow hell. Just a long slab of black asphalt bordered by rock and dust and two dry ditches. Every minute or so, a car sped past and we moved closer to the ditches.

We passed an entrance to another subdivision but didn't enter.

"It's the same as the other," Harold said. "It doesn't lead anywhere."

After an hour or so we came to the first building we had seen on the farm road. It was a strip mall comprised of a gas station, a movie-rental store, and a pizza delivery shop. A suburban outpost with all the essentials. Most of the group walked into the gas station to refill water bottles. Harold and I stood outside. I took off my bag and lifted the shoes from around my neck. Harold touched my arm and pointed to a disheveled man peeking into a dumpster.

"He might need shoes," Harold said. I looked at the man, bearded, dirty, and, for all I knew, extremely dangerous. Then I looked at Harold.

"I don't think so."

"Try."

"I don't want to."

"Okay then, don't," he said. And somehow he won the argument. I took my shoes and shuffled over to the man, still picking through the trash.

"Excuse me," I said. He turned around, looking sheepish and surprised. I guessed him to be my age, but with the beard and the dirt, it was hard to tell.

"Here," I said, holding out the shoes. "I thought you might need these."

He examined them for a moment or two before answering. "No thanks," he said.

"I'm giving them to you," I explained.

"That's kind and all, but I don't need them." He started to turn back to the dumpster.

"These are good shoes," I said. He turned back around.

"I'm sure they are, but I'm fine."

"They're leather." I pushed them a little closer to him.

"I don't want your shoes, okay?"

"Take them. Yours are crap."

"Screw you."

"Screw me? Screw you."

That's when he hit me. Then I hit back. In a second Harold was between us. The other guy walked off, turning around every few steps to yell something about "fucking yuppie shoes."

"Better luck next time," Harold said. I picked up my shoes, tossed them into the dumpster, and went inside the gas station to get ice for my bottom lip.

The Hot Tub Incident

One night, early in the walk, we had the luxurious luck of happening upon an unwatched apartment hot tub. My feet and back have never been so grateful.

The five of us sat for an hour in that bubbling tub, talking about movies, camping trips, how little of high school algebra we remembered. Eventually Irma and Gilbert headed back to our makeshift camp in an empty lot. Shael climbed out soon after, her body steaming as I stared. Harold saw me and winked.

We soaked, chatting about nothing, watching the dark sky.

"You know my favorite concert ever?" I said. "A James Taylor concert I went to in college. I was there with a girl I was seeing and some friends from the fraternity. We were all stoned. He was too, I think. It was great. It was as close to a spiritual high as I ever had."

"Music is like that."

"But I don't even like James Taylor. I hate James Taylor. It wasn't the music. It was the crowd and the girl and the weed. It was all of it. It was the moment."

He nodded. "Like you happen upon this secret—you're surprised to find it. So clear, so real. But you can't hold on to it or even look at it straight on. It's gone as soon as you try."

"Yes."

"And you're left without even the words to describe it, but you know it was there and it was what you are meant for."

"That's it."

"God making us hungry for God."

"I'd like to know God," I said. I said it casually, letting my hand skim the water's surface.

"You're sure?" He leaned back and looked up at the sky.

"Yeah. I want that purpose. I want to be a part of it, you know?"

"That's not God. That's just tinsel on the tree."

"Sure, okay. But I do want God."

"What does that feel like, to want God, Blake?"

"I don't know. It feels like wanting. I don't know."

"Do you want to know? Because I can show you."

"Yeah, I want to know." As soon as I said that, Harold pounced. He grabbed me by the back of my neck and pushed me under the water. The hot water jets and bubbles thundered in my head. At first I thought it must be a joke and tried not to panic. I watched the drain. A minute passed. I started to struggle. I was a strong man, but Harold had me pinned. I let go a mouthful of air. My lungs tightened and I could feel blood—blue, oxygenless blood—scream through my heart. I threw out my arms, grabbing and clawing. I scratched Harold's hand and saw his blood cloud the churning water. But Harold didn't loosen his grip. My throat tensed and my head pulsed. I knew I couldn't hold out much longer. I knew I would try to breathe in the water. My body was going to suck in no matter how hard I tried to tell it not to. I was going to drown, thrashing away like one of my kittens. Harold let my ears above the water. My mouth and nose were still under.

"There," he said. "Like you want your next breath. That's how it feels to want God." Then I was up and gasping and crying. Harold leaned back. That was the first time it occurred to me that this walk might end poorly.

Relic

I paint with the basement's weak watercolors. I wait for Peter to bring me dinner. I try to guess what shade of pastel his sweater will be. It was purple yesterday. I pretend not to notice when the other Pastels bring people to the door and let them peek through the window at me.

They haven't killed me. They haven't called the police. They just look at me. I'm beginning to suspect they're proud to have me. Like a relic. A holy artifact. Powerful stuff. It makes a place a smidge more holy, gives a church something to brag about. Of course the Pastels can't brag too much about me without losing me. Most of the world wants me dead. Which is fine. I will be soon enough.

Peter treats me like a relic. Impersonal and polite. I try to speak with him.

"I want to thank you for taking such good care of me," I said.

"No need. I'm paid well."

No smiles from Peter, but he always brings my meal. Always sees to my needs. Brings me paper so I can confess.

Peter must be in his early twenties. Beddy was about the same age. Peter is more clean-cut and has gray eyes, but I could imagine him as Beddy. Let that hair grow out a little, get him to smile more. He could be Beddy.

Beddy

We met Beddy our first week of walking. Most meals during the walk consisted of a loaf of bread, a can of soup, maybe some cheese. But every now and then we treated ourselves to a Waffle House. Harold believed Waffle Houses to be holy. The smell of grease was incense, the sizzle of eggs and bacon was the murmuring of angels. He loved the jalapeños they'd put in his hash browns. Loved the artificial butter spread for the waffles. And there wasn't a waitress who served us that Harold didn't feel he could marry.

He loved the clientele—ragged people sitting one to a booth, often poor, some crazy, others just lonely. Groups as well, laughing and sipping coffee and watching the cooks drop eggs onto the grill, scatter potatoes, lay a thin steak next to it all. It smelled sweet, smelled brown. No matter what time of day or night, the Waffle House smelled of breakfast and Harold saw breakfast as a meal of hope.

"Lunch is a meal of necessity. Dinner is a meal of remembrance. But breakfast is hope and there's nothing tastier."

That day, though, was a headache day for Harold. He ordered no food, just coffee. He said nothing, lost in the coffee, adding more cream and studying the spirals, just as he had on his last day in the office. Shael occasionally put her hand to his neck, and he would look up and smile, but he'd soon return to the coffee. I remembered what he had said about his migraines, how the mirrored hole slowly filled his sight, and I knew each time he looked up he saw less and less of us.

In the made-for-television movie, *Harold Be Thy Name*, he's always moving, frantic and very alive. But there were hours or days of slowness that he slipped into. Sometimes this just meant he was a little low, a little less energized. Other days it meant he wouldn't say a word to anyone.

While walking his moods set the pace. Some days the others and I would have to jog to keep up. Then there'd be days when we wouldn't walk at all. We'd stay in some campground and Harold would wander off and sit alone for hours.

That morning we sat around Harold and his coffee. The rest of us ate omelets and hash browns, talking about the ending of *It's A Wonderful Life*. I looked at the sky and tried to guess whether it would rain.

That's when I saw Beddy in the parking lot. He crawled down from the passenger side of an eighteen-wheeler's cab and tossed his pack over his shoulders. His hair covered his ears and hung down around his eyes, and he hopped a little as he walked.

The moment Beddy pushed through the Waffle House door, Harold woke up. It was always sudden, like the weather breaking. He raised his head and chuckled a little.

"Feeling better?" Shael asked.

"Much." He sipped his coffee.

Beddy glanced around the room. His eyes fixed on Harold, who had his back to him.

"Hey, what are you doing here?" he said from the door, laughing, and bounced to our table. When Harold turned, I could see that Beddy had made a mistake. "I don't know you, do I?"

Harold shook his head and invited him to pull up a chair. Beddy sat his lanky body down and rubbed his eyes.

He looked hungry, a little worn down. But when the waitress asked what he wanted, he just ordered water.

"Are you sure?" Harold asked. "It's on us."

"I don't even know you."

"That's less than important."

"Well, okay." He smiled and ordered a waffle and eggs.

"Been traveling long?" I asked.

"Since California."

"What brings you to Texas?" Gilbert asked.

"Oh, you know, life, looking."

Beddy had left a brother in Santa Cruz, called to Texas by a dollar bill pinned to the ceiling of a coffee shop. "Each bill has something written on it. Ever seen that? Stuff like 'Johnny loves Jane' or 'Class of 2010' or whatever and some one sticks it up. But the one right over my head, I mean a direct shot, says 'You have to go to Texas!' So I think 'Hey, I'll go to Texas.' My brother wanted me to stay with him. Said he could get me a job selling barrels. But the bill had spoken.

"So I left the next day in this old clunker of a car. No AC, wouldn't go over seventy, and half the time it just wouldn't start, but man, I loved that car. Tires so thin you could feel the road change texture. The thing couldn't climb a hill without slowing down to twenty-five. And so loud, that engine all rumbling and bumping, so loud I could sing and not hear myself. Couldn't hold a grudge against that car. It carried me up and up to the top of the ridge, to places where you can see for years. You understand?"

We nodded, watching him lean forward to us and bounce in his chair. His breakfast arrived, but he never slowed his story, somehow aiming the words past the mouthfuls of food. "That sun, hiding behind those mountains like some shy child. I mean, holy. And the sunlight in the morning, orange-yellow morning glow, filling the car until you think you can breathe it in. Sometimes I'd roll down the window just to let more in or feel the temperature change from state to state or hour to hour. All that change in one day."

"So how long did it take you?" Gilbert asked.

"To get to Texas? A while, once the car died." he said. "It just didn't want to go anymore. I stayed with it for a day or two, next to a rock hard sandcastle cliff out in Utah, all brown-orange and lonely. Everything's old in Utah, everything stretching up, out, and back. It was good lonely, still hurts, still hollow, but being lonely in a beautiful place is finer than being lonely on my brother's couch."

An Introduction to Haroldism
Solo Pilgrimage

According to the Third Conference for Haroldistically Sympathetic Churches, a devout Haroldian should aim to take two pilgrimages in his or her life. One is with a community. The other journey is made alone. The solo journey has no rules. Some make it a weekend hike. For others the journey takes years. Thousands of people choose to make the pilgrimage by retracing the steps of the founder of the rite: Bedrick (Beddy) Hobbleton. His route from Santa Cruz, California, to Rosenberg, Texas, has become one of the most frequented pilgrimages in the world. Those who travel it are affectionately called "Bedheads."

There are several excellent texts to guide you if you plan on making the journey, including *The Genuine Journey, Hobbleton's Travels*, and *The Bedhead Cruz: A Complete Guide from Maps to Prayers*.

Bedheads have become a major industry for Santa Cruz, and a pilgrim should be wary of the "essentials" local vendors advertise. Many overeager travelers are duped into paying high prices for poor quality used cars that are "guaranteed to break down in Utah!" It is rumored that dealers retrieve the abandoned cars along the route and tow them back to Santa Cruz, only to make quick repairs and sell them again.

Of course, there is no way to know the exact route Beddy Hobbleton actually took, and there is much debate over the subject. Nevertheless, one route has become the most popular with Bedheads.

Take Route One up the coast to San Francisco. Once there, take IH 80 to Fairfield, then State Highway 12 west until it hits 88 just outside of Lodi. Follow that west until you reach US Highway 50. This will be your road through Nevada and Utah.

There are some highlights along the route: Austin, Nevada, with its popular hostel and yearly folk festival; Great Basin National Park; and the aptly named Confusion Mountain range in Utah. Many believe it was in this desolate region that Beddy's car was abandoned, but some claim it was further east. Whatever the facts, this section of desert with its howling winds and rocky terrain has become a popular place for meditation and prayer.

Traveling by foot and hitchhiking, Beddy most likely made his way through the rest of Utah and into Colorado along IH 70. It is believed that in Grand Junction his journey again followed Highway 50. Many Bedheads pause in Montrose, Colorado, to carve their names in one of the trees of Mesa Verde National Park as it is believed Beddy did during his travels.

The path continues east along Highway 50 until Pueblo, Colorado, where it turns into south IH 25. In Raton, New Mexico, the path leads west along Highway 87 through Clayton, New Mexico, home of the Hobbleton Museum. Highway 87 takes you into Texas and through to Amarillo, Texas. From here, Highway 287 leads into Dallas where it is thought Beddy applied for work at The Sixth Floor Museum dedicated to the assassination of President John F. Kennedy. He was not hired. IH 45 leads to Houston and Highway 59 to the now famous Waffle House of Rosenberg, Texas.

Along the route to Texas, you will find no end to restaurants and hotels catering to the Bedhead market. Hundreds display signs claiming "Beddy slept here" or "Beddy ate here." It has been noted that if Beddy Hobbleton had slept and ate at every establishment that claims him, it would have taken him over two years to reach Texas. By most accounts he was on the road for just under five weeks before meeting Harold.

As We Walked

So many miles. So many steps. Such a simple thing can carry you for such a long way. We avoided the direct routes. Harold led us down back roads, through small towns, across farmland, only occasionally touching major highways. Hardly ever a straight line.

"Maybe a map would help," Gilbert said.

"It's not about maps," Harold answered. "It's about muscles. We're learning how to walk."

We could feel our calves harden and our backs growing stronger than the strain. We slept outside, next to a plastic playscape, under a bridge, on the groomed grass of a golf course. We tossed through night-noises: passing cars, barking dogs, squirrels rustling tree branches. We woke in blind darkness feeling bugs crawling on our faces, but it was only our sweat or the wind. We blinked our eyes open to stillborn pale dawn. Then, as if someone had slapped breath back into it, the sky would glow pink.

I remember Gilbert as he walked rattling on about the evils of government control and taxes. Shael smoking and quiet. Irma humming. Beddy whistling, hopping up and down. Harold in front, his red poncho hanging from his arms like unused wings.

From the beginning, I missed my wife and daughter. Missing them was the closest I'd felt to them in years.

On our ninth day it rained. A cool rain that bounced off our faces. We could smell the clouds, smell the electricity of the sky. How long had it been since we had not run from rain, not thrown an umbrella or newspaper over ours heads and dashed for shelter?

Then it was over, a brief cloudburst, and the sun came out, heating the air and ground. In the warmth the ground gave up all its history in rich, muddy aromas. We could smell its layers, its rot, its roots and worms and stones and growth. The hot air drifting up pant legs, squeezing past buckles and billowing into shirts, gathering at necklines, and puffing through like invisible steam with all the smells of the earth. A smell so strong we held our breath.

The Girl I Never Made Love To

My mind wandered as we walked, just bouncing around inside my head. It's the same inside this basement. I think about things I haven't thought about in years. Some things I haven't wanted to think about in years, other things just got lost in the shuffle.

Maybe it was Beddy's youth, or maybe I was feeling younger, but during those first few days of walking, I kept thinking about my high school sweetheart: Jessica Waller. She was treasurer of the student council, listened to country music, had hazel eyes and a slightly crooked nose. For years after, a whiff of the peach-syrup perfume she wore would make my crotch ache.

We'd park near the baseball fields in my mother's beige Cadillac, trying to get at something. Me rubbing on the outside of her shirt and counting off thirty seconds until I tried for under the shirt. Careful now, be subtle, keep the kissing going. Of course, how subtle can a seventeen-year-old boy be? How subtle did she want me to be? Even then I knew this backseat dance was a ritual that had been performed a million times. Something my father must have done and my grandfather and my great-grandfather. A rite of passage, a thrilling and embarrassingly clumsy exploration.

That summer, before my senior year, Jessica and I spent our days at Lake Ray Hubbard. Her dad owned a jet ski and we'd tow it out and ride the choppy waters, the sun baking our shoulders and noses. And if the shore was quiet, or if the jet ski stalled in the waves and we were left standing up to our chests in lukewarm water, we'd go to pressing against each other. Laughing. I named her breasts Bert and Ernie. She named part of me Big Bird. And I was eager as hell to reach her Grover.

Grover worked as a name, but secretly I thought of her warmest spot, always hidden behind humid panties, as Oscar's trashcan. That strange, unseen realm from which Oscar produced toys, food, furniture. Always amazing, Oscar would disappear into his can and you could hear his feet descending a long staircase, make out the rattling of junk, before seeing him emerge again with some found wonder. That's where I wanted to go. But I was still only bluntly caressing cotton, my hand shaking at the nest-like texture of the hairs I wasn't quite yet allowed to touch. Soon, I knew, I would. I would stay the course, run the race. I knew she would be my first and I would be hers.

Jessica had to go to a church summer camp for a week in July, and we were both dreading the time apart. The night before she left, my hand slipped under the panties and my fingers first encountered that dreamy wetness. I saw her off the next day and she cried a little.

"And Grover will miss you too," she whispered in my ear, and I blushed. I had never understood longing until that week apart, that interruption of our months of foreplay. I spent my time imagining places we could be alone, hidden rooms with soft pillows and a stereo. I must have deflowered her a thousand times in my mind, mixing what I knew of her body with images I'd seen in contraband porn magazines. I was ready to explode by the time she returned.

"I've got so much to share with you," she told me in the church parking lot. I thought I knew what she meant, knew what she wanted to share. I was wrong.

"I've fallen in love with Jesus," she said once we were in the car. I laughed at the phrase, but she only stared back with complete sincerity.

That night, over hamburgers and cokes, she told me all about Jesus. How good he was. How he had died for her sins. How she had "accepted him into her heart." I nodded along. It sounded like pretty standard church stuff. It wasn't till later in the back of that trustworthy Cadillac, my hand palming Ernie, that she told me that Jesus would want us to "slow down the kissing stuff."

I was naturally concerned, but I smiled and removed my hand, silently wondering how long this inconvenient development would last. As it turned out, it lasted a very long time. Jessica, who had been only nominally involved with her church, was now a regular attendee. Youth group pizza parties or overnighters became higher priorities than trips to the lake with me. And the we-should-slow-down conversation was becoming a common post-make out event.

Jessica was conflicted. A battle waged in her deepest parts between her newfound faith and every single bubbling hormone in her body. For me there was no conflict at all. Jesus is fine, but sex is better. We still rubbed, touched, pressed, but I had to be more subtle, more seductive, counting higher and higher before letting my hands proceed.

"No," she'd say, pushing my hand away. "That's too far."

"Okay," I'd say and return to my counting, gently pushing her boundaries out and out towards that distant coast.

She enjoyed our steamy encounters, but afterwards she'd be bombarded with guilt. Jesus moving as subtly and seductively as me, but pushing her boundaries in the opposite direction—further inland. He showed her verses in her pink-leather bible or spoke to her through her youth group leader, an overly enthusiastic twenty-two year old saving up for seminary.

"He sees us, you know," she said one night when I had managed to get her shirt all the way off. "He's watching right now."

"What a pervert!" I said. That lost me ground.

Over the next few months, I progressed bit by bit. It was exciting, dangerous. Hours were spent in that Cadillac, pushing ourselves forward. Then she would feel guilty and I would comfort her, and then we would begin pushing again. Slowly moving forward, onward, eyes on the prize. But at the final border, Jesus stonewalled us. There was orgasm, at least for me, soiling my jeans. But those panties stayed on and true intercourse, Jessica assured me, would not happen until she was a married woman. That's what Jesus demanded.

Her language gave our virginity eternal significance. We were daring damnation. Heaven and Hell witnessed our groping, took sides, and cheered or jeered.

I pushed the battle out of the backseat and waged war against the man himself. With teenage logic and passion, I argued that the suffering in the world proved that no god existed.

"That's people's doing, not God," she protested.

"Why doesn't He help?"

"Free will, our free will. People don't follow Him and there's suffering," she said with a condescending shrug. "No Jesus, no peace. But know Jesus—that's know with a 'k'—and know peace."

This, I knew, was a one-liner she had heard from her youth group leader.

"So God just watches their suffering and then sends them to Hell?" I asked.

"They choose Hell by not choosing Jesus."

Another brilliant one-liner. He had also taught her such gems as, "His pain, your gain" and "Jesus was asked how much he loves the world, and Jesus said 'This much.' He spread out his arms as far as they'd go and died."

My favorite was: "If you were the only person in the universe, Jesus would still die for you."

"If I was the only person in the universe, who would nail him to the cross?" I countered.

"Well," she looked worried. "I guess you would."

I should have listened to that.

Of course, none of my arguments worked. She explained how I couldn't understand. I didn't have Jesus in my heart, so my judgment was flawed.

We dated our entire senior year, coming so close to sex that someone watching would have a difficult time discerning whether or not coitus had been achieved. But we never crossed that line.

When I finally did lose my virginity my first semester of college, to a girl more than willing, it was a let down. A quick rumble-tumble with an anticlimactic climax. I missed the thrill of taboo, of creatively pushing the line without actual penetration. And I missed the audience. God wasn't watching me anymore, and I was disappointed.

So I thought of Jessica while walking. I thought about her being married. I had heard she married the youth leader and had four kids.

She's old now, of course. Maybe dead. I'd like to write her. Tell her I was thinking of her. Tell her that not having sex with her was the best sex of my life.

The Bath Tub Incident

Today I couldn't get out of the bath. I tried, but my arms buckled and I splashed backwards and under. It was the hot tub all over again, except God was using age to hold me down instead of Harold. I pushed myself above the surface and called for Peter. He was there in less than a minute. With professional efficiency he lifted me from under my arms and sat me on the commode. He handed me a towel. I think my nakedness, or maybe my helplessness, embarrassed him. He tried not to look. I don't blame him. I try not to look too. I have de-evolved into a mole. A tall, lank mole that can't dig. I can't escape. I can't stab anyone's neck. I'm weak. I'm the mole in the Mole Hole. I thanked him for the help.

"Just doing my job," he said.

I asked him how long he had been a Haroldian.

"I'm not," he said. "I just work for them."

"Do they know you're not a believer?" I asked while pitifully trying to dry my back.

"It was a job requirement," he said as he took the towel and patted my back.

"Did they think if you were a believer, I would be too much of a distraction?"

"I think they were afraid I'd hurt you. Most people here," he glanced up to the ceiling, "would love to hurt you." Peter hung the towel on a hook. "I'll get you a robe."

Possum

Irma didn't like me. She wasn't rude exactly, but she wasn't nice either. For the most part she ignored me. So I kept my distance.

I usually walked with Gilbert. Irma didn't seem too wild about him either. She thought he was crude and a bragger, which he was, but that was his charm. I liked his stories about sexual escapades with young divorcees, his rants against union leaders, his claims that the Masons use the credit card companies to control population growth. I liked the way he told us the workings of his body as if he were reporting the weather. "Oh, my colon is acting quirky," he'd say. "Chances are it won't settle down till tomorrow afternoon."

We were on the outskirts of Clarkston, ten days walk from Figwood, making our way along a two-lane farm road with flat fields on either side, when Gilbert announced, "Goddamn blue jeans are chafing my nuts." He stopped walking. "I can't do this. Hold up. Ladies, keep your eyes to the road," he said, taking his jeans off and hanging them over his shoulder. "Men, I advise you not to look either. Envy, I am told, is a sin."

"You're not wearing underwear?" I asked.

"Never. Waste of fabric." He pulled his shirt as low as it would go, put his shoes back on and continued walking. Thankfully, the shirt was long enough to keep Gilbert respectable, but only just. The hemline hovered in the middle of his pale thighs like a curtain waiting to be raised.

"Put your pants on, child," Irma said, without looking back.

"I'm fine, I'm decent."

"Harold," Irma said. "Shouldn't the man have pants?"

"I don't mind," he said.

"See. I'm fine. It's like a man-dress," Gilbert said. Beddy laughed.

"Lord, forgive them," Irma mumbled.

A moment later, Shael came to a sudden halt. Harold stopped beside her. Soon we were all standing and staring ten feet ahead at a pink-nosed possum sitting on the dusty shoulder of the road. It took a few steps towards us. We all stumbled backwards and Irma squealed. The possum froze and its gray and white hairs bristled. It seemed to study us, size us up, and consider its options.

"Shouldn't it be asleep?" Beddy asked.

"Maybe it's sick," Shael said.

"Shoo," Irma said. It didn't move.

Harold moved forward, slowly.

"Careful, Harold," Gilbert said. "It could be deranged."

Harold sat down and folded his legs a few feet from the possum. Still moving absurdly slow, he put out both his hands, palms up, and laid them on the ground in front of him. The possum looked at him and squinted its red, pea-sized eyes. It wobbled forward and sniffed the air. A little closer, a step or two, and it sniffed Harold's fingers. Then it stepped onto Harold's hand and crawled up his arm, dragging its ribbed tale like a dead earthworm behind it. It curled up on Harold's shoulder and nuzzled its snout into his hair. "Who's a good possum?" Harold cooed. "You're a good possum."

This is my clearest image of Harold. Sitting on the side of the road in his baggy red poncho and smiling like he'd brought peace to the world by befriending a possum.

The moment was short-lived. A police car pulled up behind us with its lights flashing. The possum, spooked by the lights, flexed its claws and, using Harold's scalp for leverage, propelled itself into the group. We went screaming in every direction. The police, seeing us scatter, jumped from their car and yelled for us to freeze. We froze.

"Hands above your head!" one cop yelled. Unfortunately, with his arms raised, Gilbert's shirt was no longer covering what it had once been covering.

"Oh, Christ," said the other cop.

"Yes?" replied Harold, blood dripping from his face. At this point, I knew that we were going to jail.

Another police car slammed to a halt next to the first. While the rest of us were being frisked, Gilbert was told to wrap a blanket around his waist.

"Why don't I just put my pants back on?"

"Sir, I don't see how you can do that without exposing yourself again."

"Ah, you're flattering me."

"Just use the blanket, sir."

We were detained on "suspicion of vagrancy" and taken downtown. Not that the town of Clarkston had much of a down to speak of.

"You know my lawyers can eat your ass, don't you? They can eat you," Gilbert said from the backseat. He, Harold, and I were in one patrol car. Irma, Shael, and Beddy were in another.

Harold kept his face to the window, but I could tell he was pleased with himself. And although I wouldn't show it, I was loving it too. I loved the look of the wire mesh between me and the cops and being on the wrong side of it. I loved the crushed feeling in the backseat. I loved how it started to rain as we drove through the small town. I was being taken in. I was an outlaw.

It wasn't much of a jail. Two cells with two sets of cots. We were the only ones there. They put the men in one cell, the women in the other. They were generous, lending us extra blankets and bringing in burgers and fries for dinner. I was disappointed. I had been ready to righteously suffer in the hands of unjust authorities. Instead it was the most comfortable we'd been in days.

After the others in my cell had fallen asleep, I sat against the wall, next to the bars. A single florescent light over the door that led out to the desks flickered and made a quiet buzzing sound. It was like the light that had been above my cubicle, the fake white light that lit my days for so many years. Too clean, too unreal. The NutraSweet of lights.

"Is anyone awake over there?" I heard Irma ask from the other side of the wall.

"Just Blake," I whispered.

"Oh." She was hoping for someone else.

"Don't you hate florescent lights?" I asked.

"Humph," she said.

"It's got be a health hazard."

"Humph."

"Irma, you don't like me, do you?"

After a long pause, she answered, "Not much."

"Why? Because I'm white?"

"It's not about who you are," she said. "It's about how you treat me. Or treated me. You don't get to treat me anymore."

"I paid you well." As I said it, I wished I hadn't.

"I hated your neighborhood. Ladies explaining how to mop and how to use the washing machine, speaking slowly as if I had no kind of mind. Children seeing me like a pet. You and your wife. Calling me by my first name, but I called you by your last name. Never once did you invite me to use your first name. Even your little girl could call me by my first name. I bet I'm the only adult in the world she doesn't respect enough to call Mrs. That or Mr. This. And I know I'm the only black person who has ever stepped into that house." She paused for a moment, maybe giving me a chance to correct her. I didn't.

"I'm going to tell you something now and you're not going to like it, but I'm going to tell you anyway. A few months ago I was on my way to clean your house. Your wife asked me to come an extra time that week because you were going to have a dinner party. I stopped at the HEB to get some bleach for the whites, " she laughed a little. "Bleach for the whites. That's funny. Anyway, I was in one bad mood. My plumbing wasn't working and my grandson was sick. I'd been up half the night at my daughter's apartment. She was staying home with the boy, so I knew I'd have to clean her houses too. It was the pretty HEB I went to, the one near your house. Same name as the one on my side of town but cleaner and nicer and the fruit ain't rotting. I was just mad and tired and felt like dying or killing. Yeah, killing was sounding pretty good. The whole aisle of cleaning products was temptation. Just a spoonful in your coffee or milk, you know? And all the names had new meanings. Shout, Gain, Cascade, Cheer. So I started filling up my cart, piling up all those pretty bottles. I got lots of bleach, 'cause it makes whites whiter."

She let out a low chuckle and took a deep breath. I didn't make a sound. "Ah, I know I was acting crazy, but I was feeling happy and whistling. Then I turned into the frozen food section, and there's this girl handing out samples of little sausages. I popped one in my mouth and swallowed. That's when I felt the cutting in my throat. And the girl says, 'Ma'am, we have a little trash can for the toothpick.' And I just knew it. God was punishing me for all my hate, punishing me with the toothpick and sausage in my throat. I couldn't even breathe. And I looked around at all those smiley white people and walked away with my cart. I was not going to die begging them for help. I knew I was going down, but I was going to keep my pride. Now, my throat was really hurting, but I hid it, even when it started tensing up and twitching. I started crying but kept wheeling the cart and gripping the handle with all I had. But I lost my legs and fell down. The cart came with me and all those colorful bottles went spinning. A bottle split open and some thick, blue detergent oozed out. People came running and slipped on the stuff and fell all over the place like they were dancing. It was funny. My ear was pressed against the floor so when they fell it was like thunder in my brain. I could see them all staring and scared 'cause I was turning so pale. I think they were afraid I was turning white, that's what I think. I was ready to die. Ready to let it go. But before I could, I saw Harold kneeling over me. I promise I knew then and there. 'It's Jesus,' I told myself. 'Jesus is in the HEB store.' And Harold put a hand on my cheek and just like that I could breathe. Then he left and I didn't see him again until the day I quit your house."

"You think it was a miracle?" I asked.

"Oh yes. Yes, for sure," Irma said. "It was a miracle for you and me. A toothpick saved you. Harold saved me."

"Maybe you just swallowed it."

"No, sir. It was a miracle. And I can still feel that toothpick, all the time. I feel it right now. It's a reminder in my throat."

It was quiet again. The florescent light flickered. Sick light.

"You still want to kill me?" I asked.

"Not usually," she said.

I wanted to tell her I was sorry. I felt like I should. I also wanted to tell her to stay the hell away from my family. That felt right too. I didn't do either. Instead I told her I had drowned some kittens in a sink. She hummed a little.

Sitting there, my back to the cell wall with Irma on the other side, was like church. Like what I imagine a Catholic feels in confession. But we were just two penitents. No priest.

"Goodnight, Blake."

"Goodnight."

Mother Irma

I sing in praise of Irma. She was rich. Strong. A mother who could hurt and comfort.

She cherished transparency. That's why she and Gilbert got along. At first it seemed they would hate each other. They disagreed on almost everything. But neither flinched at speaking out and they both respected that.

After Harold's death, she kept walking. Town to town, stopping at churches and talking about Harold, spreading the word. Her own church turned against her. But she never turned against them. That's how she won. Never intending to defeat anyone, she crumbled the Baptists.

She died while walking through a small town in Kansas. There's a grave on a farm that people visit. I did once, late at night. Even from her grave I could feel her condemning and condoling.

Her daughter Lo-Ruhamah wrote a biography and made enough money to retire and never clean a house again. The title of the book is *Mother of the Faith*.

She wanted to kill me. She loved me dearly. Mother Irma, blessed be your name.

First Words

The next morning I woke to Harold's laughter. He sat with crossed legs on the cell floor speaking through the bars to a woman with a bird-like face and pad of paper.

"No, no cause. Just walking."

"But why?"

Harold paused. "We don't know yet."

She scribbled down his every word.

"The paper comes out every Tuesday. I could send you a copy?"

So the *Clarkston Weekly Eagle* earned the honor of printing the first report of Harold Peeks. The seventy–word article, titled "Man and Others Walk," ran right under a piece on Girl Scout Cookies and a feature on that year's creek cleaning plans.

"We might even run a picture. Can I take some pictures?" She pulled a small camera from her purse and Harold smiled as she clicked.

Hiding

Sleeping in the jail cell was the safest I'd felt since we'd left Figwood. A part of me wanted to stay. Sleep on the cot, wait for the nice policemen to bring me fast food, hardly walk a step all day long. But we were gone by noon.

I never grew completely accustomed to sleeping outside. Sounds would startle me, wake me. I imagined drunk hicks beating me in my sleeping bag or waking up to find an animal chewing my face. And a more sinister fear. I'd sit up sweating, sure that we were being followed, pursued. Something was hunting us. I tried to tell Harold.

"We should hide more," I said. "We're too exposed at night."

"Come on, Blake. You spent enough time hiding." He put an arm around my shoulders. "Most of America is hiding. And most people couldn't even say what they're hiding from."

"What are they hiding from?"

He looked at me as if he were surprised I didn't know.

"Me, of course," he said. "I'll gobble them down like pretzels."

Peter and Prayer

"You look worse," Peter told me, pulling the sheets off my cot and replacing them with clean ones.

"I'm half-dead," I said. I was sitting in front of my notepads.

"How's the writing?"

"Ups and downs."

"I tried praying last night," he said, standing with a ball of my laundry.

"How was that?"

"Uneventful."

He turned and began making my bed with a clean sheet. I thought about his neck. I thought about my sharpened paintbrush. I thought about running out the door.

When he leaves and locks the door, I return to my writing.

I will kill Peter.

I write it, but I don't believe it.

I will kill Peter.

Still don't believe it.

I will kill Peter. I will ram this paintbrush into his neck.

Better. Details help.

I will kill him. I will kill him. I will kill him.

Sometimes you have to write something over and over before it becomes true. That's how America became great and later, after his death, how Harold became God.

Beddy's Bible

We were cutting through a field of waist-high grass, like Smurfs through shag carpet. It was an unseasonably warm December day. The sun, hot and white, pushed the humid air down and around, packing us in. Beside me, Beddy flipped through a worn brown binder. He pulled out a postcard and handed it to me. A picture of a swimming hole shaded by live oaks. I read the back.

Beddy—

Ate plantains for breakfast and went swimming in a limestone pool. The water is cold and wonderful. There's music everywhere. Why don't you come? You could stay the winter. They've got bats here. They'd love to see you too. I'm happy but I miss you everyday.

Love, Lisa

"Did you go?" I asked.

"No."

"Maybe she's still there."

"She got married and moved to Costa Rica," he said. "I missed that one." He took the postcard and placed it inside the brown binder. I had seen Beddy's binder before, often tucked under his arm or open on his lap. It was the cheap kind. Cardboard with a faux-leather covering that was peeling at the corners.

"What is that?" I asked. Beddy smiled shyly.

"It's my bible," he said, holding the binder in both hands and studying its blank cover. "I've been collecting it for years." He handed it to me. "As I see it, God's hidden little bits of scripture all over the world so you have to keep your eyes open."

It was stuffed with torn pages from novels, war photos from magazines, a wrinkled grocery list, a smooth piece of beach glass in a ziplock bag, sheet music from *Porgy and Bess*.

"You know Matthew Arnold, the poet?"

I shook my head.

"Great stuff. I'm adding it," he said in a whisper, as if he were telling me a secret. "I'm starting to get the poetry thing." Beddy let his hands brush the tops of the grass. "In school they had only half the story. They said poets fly, that's what they got right, but they were always teaching me how to watch, how to see them looping and everything—but that's not the point. Matthew Arnold doesn't want me to watch, he wants me to climb on his back and go flying with him. He wants me to get high up there and look down on the world in a way I never have. Just looking and floating 'til you forget the poet. Don't watch him, watch the view, you know?"

"So why these things? Why do you keep them?" I asked, flipping through a garage sale flyer and a set list for a band I'd never heard of.

"I guess it's like God is holding the world and these are the places his fingers are touching."

"They're holy or something?"

"Everything's holy," he said.

"Then why not just call everything your bible?"

Beddy grinned. "Blake, you'll be a mystic yet."

Whisper in Corners

"Excuse me, Mr. Peeks?" He was leaning across the front seat of his Volvo Wagon and peering at us through the passenger side window. We stood on the shoulder of a two-lane blacktop, our legs burning from the day's walk. "You are Harold Peeks, aren't you?"

Harold leaned against the door and smiled into the car. "That's me."

"Well, cool," he said, smiling. "I've heard of you." He lifted his cell phone and snapped a picture of Harold. "Ah, have a good walk, I guess." He gave a little wave and pulled away.

Gilbert brushed the dust from his pants. "What an asshole." But Harold only grinned.

"How did he know you?" I asked.

Harold shook his head. "Best way to spread a secret? Whisper in a corner and wait for the echo," he said.

Others stopped us on occasion. "Are you that Harold guy?" "Hey, Mr. Peeks!" Sometimes Harold would slow and chat for a while. Other times he nodded and walked on.

In Bryerton, a woman ran out of a gas station waving us down. "Harold Peeks? You're Harold Peeks."

"Nope," Harold said. "Never heard the name."

Beddy's Breathing

For Beddy breathing was prayer. He'd take time to sit or walk alone, and if you asked him what he was doing, his answer was always, "Breathing."

Beddy had a rhythm to the way he did things. The way he walked, talked, even his laughing, and I wonder if it all came from his breathing.

"Susan could breathe and listen all night long. She's the one who taught me how to do it," he once told me. We were walking along a railroad track, balancing on the rails like children.

"Susan was incredible. She had these bleached blond dreadlocks and eyes like glacier ice," he said. "And these tiny, round breasts that made me happy every time I saw them. 'Close your eyes. Keep them closed,' she'd say. 'Keep them closed for so long that the light is different when you open them again.' You sit still long enough, and you listen, but you don't sleep, you listen. It's hard to do. You calm your brain by making it concentrate on breathing. It calms your body too. Then you listen."

I asked him what he heard.

"Different days, different things," he said. "I hear wind, a lizard, a buzz, sometimes a hawk or a fly, and other times nothing at all. One of them is God."

"Which one?"

"I don't know," he said, leaping from one rail to the other. "The lizard hides in the rocks as soon as I move my head, the hawk is always above me, hunting me, and only its shadow touches me. The fly is in my ear, tickling me, too close. The wind is almost invisible, but it connects everything."

"What about the buzz?"

"The buzz is in my head. It might be mine and mine alone. It might drive me mad." He jumped back to the first rail, just catching his balance.

"I hear a buzz," I said. "Less now, but I still hear it."

He looked at me and smiled.

"I'm glad to be here, Blake. Glad to be with you," he said. "Utah was so lonely. I tried breathing out there, and all I heard was lonely."

I nodded.

"They say if you get lonely enough, God will meet you there," he said, stepping from the rail and kicking a clump of dirt. "But I'm afraid to try."

Safe Jobs

The first banks failed during our walk. We heard about it in passing conversations, discarded newspapers, overheard breakfast talk at Waffle Houses.

That was just the beginning. Soon enough jobs were lost. Not blue collar jobs . . . those were always lost. These were cubicle jobs, safe jobs, jobs that had degree requirements and a company gym. Lost. I read in the business section of a *USA Today* that Promit Computers had announced layoffs of four hundred people.

Thrack

One day Harold picked up a walking stick from the side of the road. Just an old piece of wood five feet high, an inch in diameter. He knocked the pavement with each stride.

It wasn't solid wood which would make a *swak* sound. It was shattered inside, so it rattled as it hit: *thrack*. Every step. *Thrack. Thrack.* Like a loud, splintered clock. It made my teeth hurt. Made me blink too much. *Thrack. Thrack.* After half a day I complained.

"You know what this sound is, Blake?" Harold said without slowing. "It's monotony." *Thrack. Thrack.* "This is what your life sounds like to the universe." *Thrack.*

Sometimes he was cruel. I don't know why.

He walked for another hour, then snapped the stick over his knee and threw it in the ditch.

Hands

I remember the first day they held hands, Shael and Harold. We had been on the road for two weeks. A little less than halfway to Austin. I was walking behind them, watching her tight shape, the beading sweat on the back of her neck. Catching some of the sadness that surrounded her like perfume. Day by day she walked closer and closer to Harold's side. Now each step of her steps matched his.

Shael had changed as we walked. Even I, who had hardly known her before, could see how different she was. For one, she had become more Jewish. On Fridays at sunset she took to lighting Sabbath candles and saying a quick prayer in Hebrew. She always did this alone, away from us. Often, after her little ceremony, Shael would spend the rest of the evening without saying a word. She would just sit alone, lighting cigarettes with her candles.

Arms swinging closer as they walked. Her thin fingers inches from Harold's stubby hand, almost touching, each swing a little closer. They were talking. I couldn't make out the words, but I could hear the sounds and see their heads bob. Shael tilted her head back a little, I think she laughed.

Harold often made her smile, and smiling wasn't a natural thing for Shael. She had a mournfulness about her. A guilt. I could see it in the way she smoked. Even before I knew her story, I could see that Shael thought she deserved to die. Each time she pushed the smoke through her clenched teeth you could see her guilt slightly eased. Her eyes would follow the smoke—another minute of her life, another chunk of lung. And if she had ever had pleasure from the tobacco, it had subsided to nearly nothing and left her with only addiction. Addiction to the nicotine and to the punishment.

I think it was her gloom that drew Harold in.

Their hands finally touched. Just fingers brushing. It was sweet, I suppose. But I found it inappropriate. Rude. I was alone, having to watch them come together.

She reached, encouraged by the touch, and took his hand firmly in hers.

Rude.

Here

Harold and Shael were happy and together while my wife and daughter were a hundred miles away. And I missed them, more than I knew I could. I missed Jennifer's smell. I missed Tammy's voice. I just missed them being near.

I tried calling. Almost every day. The phone would ring and ring and finally a machine with my voice would answer. I'd leave my clumsy message. "Hi. Just calling. So. I guess I'll call later or maybe tomorrow or something. I hope you're all well." Blat blat blat blat nothing to say, nothing at all blat blat blat. "Good-bye."

No matter what time of day, I always got the machine.

I wanted to be back home watching Disney films. I wanted Tammy to be six again, I wanted Jennifer and I to be in love again. I wanted to order a pizza and have all of us eat in front of the television, laughing at sitcom one-liners and inside family jokes. I wanted to cheer for Tammy's volleyball team, I wanted to compliment my wife's cooking, I wanted to set all of us down in front of the pool and take a hundred photographs. Why didn't I ever want them like this before? Why didn't they ever answer the phone?

That day, seeing Shael and Harold take each other's hand and walk like lovers just made the hurt run deeper.

I found myself asking, "Why am I here?" Repeating it, the words coinciding with my breathing and my steps. "Why am I here? Why am I here?"

I didn't have an answer. I could have stopped, could have turned around, but I had lost Jennifer. I had lost Tammy. I'd go back to Figwood, ask for my job back, move into an apartment complex, and spend my nights drinking light beer and watching sport highlights with other middle-aged divorcées, driving to Burger King at 9 p.m. because I'm out of microwavable dinners, running into my sad ex-wife and angry daughter in the parking lot, being introduced to Mitch NewGuy who slurps his Coke, shakes my hand, and wraps his arm around what was my wife. I'd nod, seeing that she isn't that sad and my daughter isn't that angry. Driving back to the apartment, the fries cold already. Pushing a half-eaten burger down the disposal, pouring some gin into a coffee cup, and raising a glass to toast freedom. I'd rather be walking.

"Why am I here?" The mantra mixed itself up, each footstep and breath making the phrase skip and rearrange. "Why am I here?" became "I'm here. Why?" and slowly became "I'm here."

"I'm here" was true. It couldn't be argued. I repeated it. Breathe in—*I'm*. Breathe out—*here*. Beddy would have been proud.

Then the words left. For a while I was walking without asking why. My feet had blisters and my legs felt knotted, but walking had a comforting kind of consistency. I didn't have to worry about what to do or where to be. I was here and I was walking. One foot, then the next. Follow those before you.

That night we slept in a graveyard. I listened to the others breathing. Sloppy, natural breathing. *If you get lonely enough* . . . I was lonely. And knowing that Harold and Shael were only tombstones away, close to each other, made me all the more lonely. But I was there. *Here*. In the lonely. Not trying to escape. In a graveyard, not trying to pretend that I wouldn't someday be lying below the grass instead of on top. I breathed. Smells of soil and trees. I was lonely and glad and here.

Burial

Early that next morning, I dug a hole and buried my credit card, my cell phone, and my watch. I had a little service and made a tiny tombstone from tree bark.

Shape

The next few days were cool and sweet. The Texas winter air was clear and had a chill that made the sky seem higher. There was less pine now, more oak, and the land rolled slightly, unlike the strict flatness of Figwood.

I could feel the journey, the walking, changing me. Changing all of us. Even Harold. He called us driftwood. Pushed along, floating, tugged by the tide, our edges worn smooth by the waves. Losing our softest spots until we each had a different shape.

Shaped by the walking, shaped by the others, shaped by Harold.

Harold shaped us by listening to us. You talked differently because of how he listened. He had the uncanny desire to understand what you were trying to say. And you found your words meaning more because his listening honored them. Words rose to the occasion.

He walked in the same way, soaking in sounds and smells. The world itself wanted to be better because of Harold's willingness to experience it. Life shimmered around him because someone was finally paying attention, someone was getting it.

He'd say, "You could drink the air today." Or "Look at all the curves. Clouds, stones. Corners are rare in nature. Corners rarely last."

He believed rabbits had secrets they would tell no one. He believed the true saints of the world were tollbooth workers who smiled. He said the only way to be forgiven is to forgive.

Sometimes he'd sit and watch the air. Under a tree, perhaps, or against a building, hardly blinking, and then he'd say, "Dust floating. That's it. That's it."

I walked near him during those clear days, and it felt good. Steps felt good. Being with the others felt good. The world seemed to have order.

Which is real? The connection I felt those days or the isolation that came later? Opposing realities. Either life has value and I'm connected, or I am alone and mean nothing. One must be an illusion. How is it I've known both?

Value

"Do you think life, in itself, has some kind of value?" Beddy asked.

"If something is valued, it's valuable. If something is loved, it's lovable. We make it so," Harold said.

"That seems backwards," Gilbert said. "You love something because it is lovable. Not the other way around."

"Maybe you're right," Harold said. "But my guess is the road goes both ways."

What Shaped Harold

Shael waited until she believed we were asleep. She crawled from her sleeping bag into Harold's. I laid there listening to their whispers, their pushed sighs, her breaths high and full.

I don't think Harold really loved Shael. Not like she loved him, at least. He never needed her. He never needed anyone. What Harold loved was her sadness. He'd gaze at her, wanting the beauty of her hurt.

Why did he find sadness beautiful? Why did beauty make him cry? His own sadness was so like joy, or maybe awe, that the two got confused. If you were near him, that sadness would find a way into you, like a slow punch to the chest. You couldn't say exactly what the sadness was or why it was, but it was a sadness richer than all the happy moments of your life.

Shael's hurt was hollow, a need. Harold's was overflowing. I suppose that is what drew them together.

Two Mirrors Dancing

At night we talked. Sometimes we had food, sometimes a campfire. We would sit and listen to all those noises the country makes after the sun goes down and ask Harold questions. What is God? What is salvation? What is life? More often than not he would turn the questions back on us. What did we think? We'd pull at ideas, stretch words, talk in circles, and confuse each other. It was a wonderful confusion. But we never found answers.

Harold once said that the questions we had asked were all the same. And that it was the same question the world had been asking for a billion years. Not just humans asking, the whole world. "And if there were an answer," he said, "do you think it could be spoken?"

Harold and Beddy would hit on a discussion that would leave the rest of us behind. They would jump from thought to thought, and I couldn't keep up or catch the rhythm. Irma would hum along. Gilbert would grunt and throw in a few words. Shael would occasionally ask a question. But mainly it was Harold and Beddy.

One night, under a large oak tree, we watched as the two threw ideas back and forth as if they were as hot as the campfire coals—holding a thought for just long enough to singe the fingers.

"So we reflect God, right? Made in His image, so polish the glass and bounce the sun. It's not us, all the light is from the same source, right? We're God mirrors," Beddy said.

"Who can tell who the mirror is? Who can tell who leads, who follows? Both?" Harold said.

"Yes! Yes! God mirrors us and we mirror God!" Beddy jumped to his feet.

"Yes! 'Forgive us as we forgive others.' How can God love your enemy if you refuse? And if you love your enemy how can God do less?"

"Okay! I see." Beddy hopped and paced around the rest of us. "But wait. Here's the question. If one reflects the other, two mirrors dancing, two reflections, then what's real?"

"The light that jumps between them."

Beddy laughed out loud and dropped down to the ground, sitting with crossed legs. He shook his head and looked up at Harold, smiling. "It's all talk, isn't it? Doesn't mean a thing."

"It's all we've got."

It was running downhill, the two of them stumbling from idea to idea, tumbling through thoughts, pausing just long enough to catch their breath, nod and smile, and sip the tea Beddy made on his camping stove. "Yeah, yeah. It's like pain," Beddy said. "Oh man, don't let me lose this pain."

The next morning, while rolling up our bags, I asked Beddy what he meant by pain.

"I hurt. You know? I see the sky or the trees and I start hurting," he said.

"Why?"

"It's like frustration, this pull in my rib cage, and I can't even voice it. But this frustration is everything I was made for, you know?"

I nodded.

"And the worst thing is that it ends, your heart stops breaking. You go out and have a beer or watch a movie, and the pain ends. Sometimes you can't even remember it."

"Yeah."

"But not for Harold. It's like he's always there, at that heartbreak place, but kind of beyond it. It's like he's at peace with frustration."

Gratitude

One morning, well over halfway through our journey, Harold offered me an apple. I accepted.

"Aren't you going to say 'thanks'?" he asked.

"Sure, thanks," I said and raised the apple to my mouth.

"I didn't grow it," he said. I lowered the apple. He smiled. "A tree did."

"I should thank a tree?"

"And the sun and rain that helped."

"Okay, thanks tree, sun, and rain."

"And the worker who picked it and washed it," he said.

"Okay. I thank them and the truck that carried it, and the store that stocked it and you for handing it to me." I took a bite, chewed for a moment. He stared at me. I stopped chewing.

"Blake, you enjoy so little because you are grateful for so little."

Harold was grateful. You could see it in the way he ate—slowly and with focus. You could see it in the way he walked, the way he listened. It was a real gratitude. A thankfulness for each little thing.

I simply consumed, usually without a thought. But after a while I tried gratitude. I took my time, used Harold's system. I held a bread roll in my hand and worked at being grateful for the grain, wheat, even the heat that baked the bread. This helped. Made me more aware. But it was the hunger that came later that taught me to be grateful for food. It was cold that made me grateful for clothes. It was loneliness that made me grateful for others.

Arousal Day

Some days while walking, I hated the sky. It put sun in my eyes, wind in my face, and denied me my God-given right to air-conditioning. It was nearly winter, but in Texas heat holds rank over the seasons. It drained me. So I was all for it when one Sunday morning, nearly three weeks out of Figwood, Harold led us into the Woodville New Life Church, the Reverend Ben Patterson presiding. The place was clean and smelled of paint and had, oh glory, air-conditioning.

The ceiling was high and white with thick wooden beams like you'd find in a ski lodge. A few red and green veils and some artificial holly hung from the beams. On one of the side walls was a nine-foot-tall statue of Christ on the cross, his ribs pressing out against his skin, his eyes gazing up with the faintest trace of eyeliner. We walked in just as a service was beginning and sat in a long wooden pew four rows from the back. There were little cushions by each person's feet, so it wouldn't hurt if we chose to pray.

The other parishioners—with babies and grandparents and finely shaped haircuts—peeked at us over their hymnals. We were, to be perfectly honest, a mess. I was wearing the same jeans I had been wearing for three days. The one other pair I had was no better. My hair was flaring up like a rat-torn bird's nest. I kept trying to push it down, but it wouldn't stay. The others looked just as bad.

The service opened with a prayer and a few announcements made by an elderly man with a wide tie.

"Remember, tomorrow night the high school youth group will be hosting a pancake dinner to raise money for their upcoming Christmas ski trip. It will be held in the gym and starts at six. And we still need volunteers for the Samaritan Soup kitchen which is now open only on Thursdays." He glanced at us and left the podium.

The choir director, a young man in a white robe, took his place and invited the congregation to stand and join him and the choir in singing. Gilbert wouldn't sing. He sat with his arms crossed like an upset child. Harold, Beddy, and Irma stood and sang with sincere enthusiasm. I couldn't tell if Shael was joining in or just mouthing the words. I sang, but quietly.

After a few hymns the congregation was told to sit down and the choir director announced that it was better to give than to receive. Two men started passing gold-colored plates up and down the pews as a teenage girl took the stage and belted out an off-key rendition of "From a Distance." At our pew, the collector hesitated before handing us the half-filled plate. He stood there, smiling nervously and watching our hands like a mother hawk. Irma dropped in a dollar.

Soon Pastor Patterson began his sermon. I recognized the minister. Not the man himself, but the type. Balding on top, cut close on the sides, big, white smile, wide-open eyes. He reminded me of my high school girlfriend's youth leader. I'm sure that even during the most mundane of conversations, he would nod as if hearing some fascinating, heart-wrenching confession. I imagine he wore pastel button-down shirts and looked awkward in shorts. I'm sure he was kind, gentle, tidy, possibly married with several children, but often mistaken for a homosexual.

"Paul tells us that we are the body of Christ." He gathered the congregation with his eyes. "So be as Jesus was. Act as he did."

Harold turned to me and grinned, "What a mad world that would be."

"And Jesus loved people because the people are the body," the minister continued. "Rich or poor," he smiled, aiming his eyes in our direction. "Clean or dirty," another smile, "employed or currently unemployed." He took a sip of water. "So even if you're not adding anything of worth to society, you are of worth to God. And he can help you turn around." Now he was looking just at us. "You can kick that narcotics habit you may or may not have. You can find a new life with a new home and a job." He smiled so big I thought his cheeks would split. In fact, I was hoping they would split.

"Ah shit, Harold, let's get out of here," Gilbert whispered.

"Don't you disrespect this house," Irma said.

"I'll wait outside." Gilbert stood up and shuffled passed us, grumbling under his breath.

"And we are all members of the body of Christ," the minister continued. "Some are eyes, some are arms, some—"

"Who's the penis?" Harold said. The people in front of us squirmed. The minister didn't seem to hear.

"Should the eyes say, 'I'd rather be a foot?' Each of us has a different role in the body of Christ."

"I want the penis role," Harold said even louder.

The minister paused. Then chuckled awkwardly.

"Harold!" Irma said, grabbing his arm.

"Sir," the minister slowly placed his palms together. "If you can't control yourself, you're going to have to leave."

"You'd cut off part of the body? You'd castrate God?"

"All right sir, you're disrupting this service. You need to leave."

Harold jumped up on the pew. "I have come to disrupt services!"

People stood and backed away. Mothers pulled their children close to their sides. Shael muffled a laugh.

"Please, Harold!" Irma pulled his pant leg. Harold looked down at her and smiled. Two men took a few steps toward us, nodding at each other.

"Your body is not all yours. Your life is not all yours. I give you a gift," Harold raised both arms to the ceiling. The two men, their eyes wide with surprise, stopped their approach. One dropped his hand to a pew to balance himself. I couldn't tell what was happening to them, but then it happened to me. Blood rushed to my crotch like it was the center of a whirlpool. I quickly folded my hands over my lap to hide the rising. Dozens of faces were blushing, men and women. The minister quickly maneuvered himself behind the podium and stared at the choir director sitting near by. The choir director stared back and crossed his legs. From the front row, an ancient man in a wheelchair softly squealed, "Jesus!" I turned to look at Irma. She was flushed, beads of sweat dotting her upper lip. This was an act of God.

"God has a new word," Harold said, his own pants popping forward. "It is the same as the old word." He pointed to the crucifix hanging on the sidewall, and I could swear that as we watched there was a slight swelling under the purple cloth painted around his waist.

"Praise the Father, Sons, and Holy Cock," Harold said. He turned and left the church, leaping along the tops of the pews.

An Introduction to Haroldism
Arousal Day

One of the most intimate of celebrations during the Festival of Wanderings is Arousal Day. Every December 9, Haroldians ponder the miracle of their own bodies. The ritual can be done alone, with a partner, or with a community of believers. Participants sit naked and study their own genitals and erogenous zones without physical contact. The act almost always results in erections (the penis, the nipples, or the clitoris) and other signs of stimulation. After a time of self-appreciation, partners or communities often move on to examining each other, again without physical contact.

The observance of this day can take place nearly anywhere: bedroom, bathroom, a park for those living in a warmer climate, or at participating Waffle Houses.

In some traditions the sexual tension is built upon until it snaps. The final result of the ceremony is sex. But many Haroldians prefer to keep the ritual chaste. In such cases, the ritual ends with the uncorking of a bottle of white wine by a predetermined participant. At the sound of the pop, all present don a simple robe and complete the evening with a glass of the white wine and occasionally some cheese.

It is important to note that there is no shame in performing this ritual on your own. As Harold himself is quoted as saying, "There is that of God in each of us, therefore masturbation is the highest form of worship."

Reverend Patterson

Gilbert hated churches. He distrusted all things organized except businesses. Businesses, he felt, were honest. Their goal was to make a profit, and they didn't pretend otherwise. Churches were less transparent in their aims and he didn't trust that.

While walking from the Woodville New Life Church, Gilbert told me he went to confirmation classes as a child. I told him I found that hard to believe.

"Shit yeah! I was thirteen and my father had me show up to each and every hour of all the classes. The final assignment was an essay. Write my own statement of faith. It was the best goddamn thing I ever wrote."

"What was it?"

"It was titled: 'Why I Don't Believe in God.'"

"So you got kicked out?"

"Hell no. The next week I stood in front of the church and received my confirmation. So if that ain't shit, I don't know what is."

Still, Gilbert was upset he'd left the service that morning and missed the action. More than once he asked Harold to repeat the miracle. "Not that I need it," he said. "I do just fine on my own."

Irma was less impressed. She walked out of that church with fists clenched.

"Harold," she said. "There's right miracles and wrong miracles, you understand? You can't disrespect a house of religion."

"It's not about religion," Harold said.

"You're the one always talking about knowing God. You can't know God without religion."

"And gravity only works for physics majors."

"I just don't see what's to be gained by getting everyone all excited and then running out of the place like a maniac," Irma said.

"They could have followed," Harold said.

That night we were huddled around a creek-side campfire miles from Woodville. Beddy heated two cans of beans, and we were passing tortillas when a man stepped into the circle of firelight. He was no longer in his clerical robe, but I recognized him. He asked if he could sit.

We watched him stiffly lower himself to the dirt as if it had been years since he last sat without the comfort of a chair or couch. His starched shirt was ripped at an elbow, and the knees of his slacks were wet with mud. He wiped the sweat from his face and smiled. It was a weak smile. A distant cousin of the engulfing grin we'd seen during the service.

"So, quite a morning, wasn't it?" he said with a light chuckle.

"I enjoyed your sermon, Reverend," Irma said.

He nodded and mumbled a thank you.

"Would you like some beans, Ben?" Harold asked.

"You know my name?"

"It was on the sign."

"Oh, yes. Of course." He coughed into his fist. "No food, thank you. I'd take some water, if you can spare it?" Beddy handed him his water bottle and he guzzled half of it down.

"My name is Harold. Harold Peeks."

"Yes, I know who you are. Or, I had guessed."

Gilbert and I exchanged a glance. Harold's eyes never left the minister.

"You're very good walkers," he said, handing the bottle back. "It wasn't easy finding you."

"Lots of practice," I told him.

"Good. That's what builds muscles. Walking the walk, not just talking the talk. Yes. Of course, my hiker friends tell me walking the wrong way is the best way to get lost." He coughed again, looked around at us, a bit embarrassed, as if reluctantly fulfilling a duty. "Of course, scripture tells us there is only one true way. One path. And that way is Jesus Christ."

He stopped and stared at the ground for several moments.

"Ben?" Harold said.

Ben placed his hands in his lap and seemed to be gathering his thoughts. "I want to know how you did what you did." His voice was quiet, stern. Almost angry.

"How do you think?" Harold said.

"I don't know."

"You don't have to know."

"Tell me," he said, the muscles in his jaw tightening.

"How did Buddha walk on water? How did Muhammad write poetry?"

"Look, I had an injury," Ben said. "My body hasn't done that . . . that thing that happened this morning in two years and . . ."

"And the doctors don't know why, and you think your wife is sleeping with the Sunday school teacher, and you squirm every time someone asks you to perform a wedding. And you're scared to death because you're unsure about everything you were once sure about."

Even in the half-light of the fire, you could see the minister turning pale. But he said nothing.

"Your sermons have promised a Second Coming. You've preached it." Harold moved closer to the fire and his face glowed. "Did you really think it would look anything like you expected?"

Ben said nothing.

"Listen," Harold said. "Hundreds of years ago a rich man hired an artist to build a huge stone chapel. The artist drew up the design and showed it to the rich man. 'It's beautiful,' the man said. 'But you need more than two columns. Two will never hold up all the weight.' The artist promised that two columns were enough, but the man demanded more be added. So the artist built the chapel with twelve columns. It stands to this day. But if you visit the chapel and study the work, you'll find all but two of the columns are an inch short of the ceiling. Two are needed. The others hold up nothing. There's your dogma."

Ben looked up, "So what do you propose? Knock down the columns?"

"Give them a push. See if they wobble."

"And if you push down one of the two that are needed," Ben said, "the whole roof will fall in."

"Good," Harold said. "You'd finally see the sky." Harold laughed. So did Gilbert.

The minister breathed a long quiet sigh and then spoke into the fire. "I fear for your souls."

"Don't," Harold said. "Ben, I am something new and something old."

"I want you to tell me you're lying," Ben said, nearly whispering.

"We'll be leaving at dawn if you want to join us," Harold said.

"Tell me you're lying, and I'll leave you alone."

"Maps and muscles, muscles and maps. You think you have one. I'm offering the other."

The minister stood up, gazed around at us all. "You people think hell is a joke? It is very real," he said. "And you are all in real danger."

"Cool down, limp dick," Gilbert said. Harold put a hand on Gilbert to quiet him but kept his eyes on Ben.

"I'll be praying for you. I really will be," Ben said. His voice was stronger now, more sure, more angry. "I don't judge you. I don't judge you at all. But God will judge you." He nodded as if agreeing with what he had said. Then he walked from the fire.

We sat watching in the weird kind of silence that only a threat of eternal damnation can bring. Gilbert tried to laugh but it didn't travel too far. Reverend Ben Patterson had left some of his anxiety behind, and it hung in the air like the smell of burnt hair.

"Are there any more beans, Beddy?" Harold asked.

"Harold, I don't get what you're doing," Irma said. The anger from earlier was no longer there.

"Irma," he said, smiling and pulling up a spoonful of beans. "You don't get what I'm doing but you follow. That's magic."

Borders on the Boundless

Late that same night, after everyone else was asleep, I woke to see Harold standing with his neck bent and his face towards the stars. He was motionless against a backdrop of swaying trees that moved like waves in the night wind. I went and stood by him.

"Blake," he said, keeping his eyes on the sky. "More stars tonight than last night."

I looked up. The Milky Way looked like a smear of light.

"All things are one," he said. "I mean physically. All goes back to one boom. All to one point. A singularity. Everything that exists was in that one point. Isn't that strange?"

A satellite floated by, like a star on a journey. Harold used his thumbs and forefingers and made a frame against the sky. He laughed a little.

"To make borders for the infinite, that's the temptation, that's the mistake," he said. "People are more awestruck by the height of a cathedral's ceiling than they are by the height of the sky. It's why we name God. Why we try to explain things. Borders on the boundless."

The irony of Harold's life is that he became those borders. It is the desire to frame the sky that has drawn people to Harold. The same desire that drew people to Jerusalem's Temple, to Buddha, to Jesus. Show us the spot, the body in which God resides. The infinite framed by the finite.

Harold referred to himself as the Son of God, he called himself Christ, but he never claimed to be God. Never said he was a unique divine incarnation. It wasn't like that walking with Harold. It wasn't God possessing Harold like some ghost. Harold was more like a pop fly on a sunny day. He was lost in the sun. You looked for him, searched for him, but all you saw was sun.

"You know, Blake, the Big Bang didn't really change things that much," he laughed, his eyes still on the sky. "Geez, I'm drunk on God tonight. I know I sound crazy, I know that. But I tell you, God was crazy first." He looked at me with his eyebrows raised. "God's insane. And in love with us." He turned his face back to the stars. "It can be very dangerous to have a crazy person in love with you."

For a while neither of us spoke. Then he looked directly at me.

"Who am I, Blake?"

"Who are you?"

"Tell me who I am. I'll believe you."

I was suddenly afraid. Like the drop in your gut when you're standing on the edge of a canyon, knowing how easy it would be to fall or jump.

"You're Harold. You're Harold Peeks."

He smiled. "God has given you that answer."

Hush

Some days I walked without saying a word. Some days the quiet was so rich, so deep down, it felt like floating. The silence I kept during that time stuck. After Harold's death, it guided me. For years, silence was often my sole companion. I walked and hid. On the run, hiding. The last years before I was brought to this basement, I lived in Mexico. I crossed the border in Brownsville, walking with the tourists. I wanted a place where I couldn't read the paper, couldn't understand the billboards. Lonely. Very lonely. No common language, no words between us. A place where I could speak and not be heard. I could listen and not understand.

I traveled past the busy border towns, through the flat northern deserts, to a small village in the mountains. I lived for a year in a cinderblock hut with a dirt floor. I'd buy food from the locals, but I was alone. Learning as little of the language as I possibly could.

After a while, the locals believed me to be holy. A hermit saint. Why else would I be alone, be silent, unless I was spending all my time speaking with God? They painted prayers on pieces of wood and metal and left them outside my door with offerings of food or a few coins. Pictures telling me what their words could not. Asking me to pray for sick parents, risky business ventures, an infertile cow. I became an expert on the lives in the village. But I imagined them all as crudely drawn cartoons, like the prayer pictures they'd left for me. I placed the drawings around the inside of my hut, leaning them against the cinderblock walls. The pictures were more real to me than the actual people living minutes away.

I did pray for them. I began to believe maybe my prayers did have a power. Maybe God did listen. Maybe God only speaks English and I had to act as an interpreter. One day, returning from the village with plastic jugs of water, I found a new painting asking me to pray for a little boy in a yellow shirt. The picture showed the boy with dark eyes and in bed, a woman crying large, blue teardrops beside him. It was hard to look at.

I prayed. On my knees. Prayers to God, to Harold, to me. The child died. I received another drawing of the same woman with the same oversized tears beside a small grave. Below her, red flames were painted.

At the top of the drawing were clouds and angels and the Virgin. The boy in the yellow shirt floated between.

They were asking me a question. Where is he now? How would I know? I could say he was happy and in peace, but maybe God was burning him for the sin of life. Maybe he simply didn't exist anymore. I couldn't say. I couldn't help. I was just another false prophet.

I painted a simple portrait of the boy smiling in the arms of Jesus. I placed it outside my door and left the town.

Driftwood

Tonight I can hardly write. Each time I try, I fall asleep.

Shael visits the Mole Hole. Heavy smoke spilling into the room from the vent. Then, like light in smoke, she's there. I paint her. Her still, with her Sabbath candles and cigarette.

I try to paint the flames as moving. Her as still. Her still.

I remember waking one cool morning in a dew-coated field. Harold and Shael's sleeping bags were empty. I crawled from my bag and walked through a wood, scratching my legs on the brush. I found them by a small lake. Shael sat on the dock while Harold swam, sending ripples over the surface. Shael didn't move. She was still. Nearly perfect. I wanted to walk from the woods and sit in the grass or on the dock or maybe even swim. But I stayed hidden in the trees.

The picture was peace, and if I placed myself in it, then the peace would be ruined. So I watched and tried to imagine being there. Could I be that still? Can I be that still? I see that lake so often, but I'm never in the picture. I'm hiding in the trees.

"My hands are not still enough to paint you," I tell her.

Driftwood, she says.

"Why do I hurt so much?"

Driftwood, she says.

"I am sorry," I say.

She smiles and floats away.

My Warmth

By the middle of December, I didn't have many clothes left. Each day I wore the same sweater, the same shirt and jeans, and my blue and yellow jacket. Eventually the jacket went as well. We were walking in a midsized town about sixty miles east of Austin. It was foggy and the air was chilled. I was all snuggled and dry in my Teflon. We passed an old man sitting on a bench. He looked cold.

"Give him your coat," Shael said to me. Another time I might have argued. But I was so hopped up on brotherly love that I took off the jacket, placed it over the old man's shoulders, and walked on with a warmer feeling of goodwill welling in my chest.

That warm feeling lasted all of seven minutes. Then I was cold and bitter. Up until then I had left things that made my pack lighter—extra socks or the shoes I never wore. But the jacket I wanted. I even considered going back to the old man and explaining it had only been a loan. But as I was working out just how to do this, a car rolled by and the little old man, wearing my blue jacket with the yellow stripes, waved from the passenger side window. The interior of the car looked warm.

That was December 16, annually celebrated as The Day of Warmth. Of course in every version of the story told, it's Harold giving his coat. In the movie *Harold Be Thy Name*, I'm not even in the scene.

Feet

The day after I gave my coat away was colder, the rain spiked with ice sharp as glass. We found an abandoned house surrounded by untended fields. Rotten wood and walls thinner than my skin, but it kept out the wind and rain, so we hunkered down.

Three rooms. A kitchen with a stained, dry sink and a gutted oven, a bedroom with nothing but springs and an old Sears, Roebuck catalog, and a bare living room. It was a wreck, smelling of wet plaster and rot, but after weeks of having nothing, very little was something to sing about.

After an early dinner, we sat around the living room, the westward windows catching the last of the day's light. We talked softly, laughing every so often. We kept our voices low. Even Gilbert was quieter. Not subdued, just quieter. We looked at each other, in each other's eyes. And that was okay. It was all right to look into each other's eyes, to hold that gaze.

Harold said the least of all of us. He just sat on the floor smiling. We stayed like that for nearly an hour. Quieter by the minute. When we finally fell silent, Harold stood and stepped outside. He came back in with a bucket.

"Rainwater," he said. He walked back to Shael and unlaced her shoes. Then he rolled away her socks and, using a cloth, he wiped her feet clean. Gilbert was sitting to Shael's left and Harold moved to him next.

I did not like this. I had no desire to expose my feet, my uncut nails and gathered funk, the smell, the calluses.

"There's nothing worth fearing. Not a thing," he said.

Shael and Irma were crying. I watched the weeping but I didn't join in. I was too distracted. Harold never changed the water. I was the last person he would come to. My feet were going to be washed with the same gray, grimy rainwater that had washed Gilbert's corns, Beddy's hangnails, and all the other feet that had come before me.

He was now washing Irma's feet. She was sitting on a crate and humming through her tears. She leaned down and touched Harold's face.

"Harold, I know this." She whispered so quietly only Shael on her left and I on her right could hear. "Is this our Last Supper? Is this goodbye?"

Shael's tears stopped.

Harold smiled at Irma. "No," he said. "We still have some walking to do."

Then came my turn and Harold kneeled by my feet. I found myself shaking my head. It was the grime, the humiliation, the disturbing image of him below me.

"Remember this, Blake. You'll need this."

I let him take hold of my feet. I let him place them in the bucket. The water was warmer than I had expected, and my feet, barely hidden by the cloudy water, wriggled. 'We're back in the womb,' my feet thought. 'It's okay,' they mewed to themselves. 'Back in the womb and ready to be born-again.'

I looked from my feet to Harold. He looked at me. There was something mournful in his face. Something he knew about me. I saw what Irma already had. Someone was going to die. The water was lying. Death was on the way, not life. If my feet had not been held down by my legs, they might have jumped from the water and run out of the room.

"I do not fear death," Irma announced. "Not mine, nor yours, Harold. My God is the resurrection. My God is the life."

Harold shook his head, his eyes on my feet. "Irma, an empty tomb is a Hollywood ending."

"What the hell are you all talking about?" Gilbert said.

"When I'm dead, burn my body or they'll waste lifetimes waiting for my corpse to twitch. That's what I ask. Burn it up."

"But Harold," Irma said, "death is swallowed up in victory. Death is defeated."

"Death doesn't need defeating."

"Spring follows winter," Beddy said, his voice quiet. I saw a smile touch Harold's face and he gave the slightest nod. He looked up, first at me and then turned to the others.

"I can't give you tomorrow. Only today."

Light

And the room changed. More than I could describe. Forgetfulness. Skewed sequence. We talked a little. I think we sang.

Was it presence? Was it whirlpools? Beddy leaned in to me. "We're breathing each other in. Breathing ourselves out." Irma would later say it was the Holy Spirit. She reached to touch the foreheads of those near her, expecting to burn her hand.

How would I paint this? How would I show this? When I was a child my father taught me to watch the stars that can only be seen from the corner of the eye, where the eyes are most sensitive to light. "You can't look directly at the star, it will disappear." And it always did, as soon as I turned my glance. I wanted to be there, to visit that star or planet that can only be seen from the side. That night. Those lights, that's what I would paint.

Whiskey

Later, when the others were asleep and Shael was smoking in the back room, Gilbert and I sat on the front steps watching stars disappear behind clouds.

"Got a little treat for the two of us," Gilbert said and pulled out a fifth of whiskey.

I said it then and I say it now, "God bless Gilbert Forncrammer."

"To a crazy bastard," he said, raising the bottle and toasting back towards the house.

"A crazy bastard," I said.

It had been weeks since I had felt that sticky burn in my stomach. It wasn't gin, but it was fine. My mind melted just a bit and I smiled. We talked about the wind, about blisters.

"Another drink?" I said.

"What the hell. I got nowhere to be tomorrow."

That sweet dizziness and loose tongue. All the world dark and blurred.

"Gilbert, how many times were you married?"

"Twice."

"Why didn't they last?" I asked and swigged.

"The first one ended like crap. I left because I thought I had fallen out of love, or some bullshit like that. But the second was worse."

"What happened?"

"I caught her with another man," he said. "She cried, begged me to stay. I left."

"Good for you."

"Good for shit. If I had half an ass I would have tried," Gilbert rubbed his scalp. "I never got the whole unconditional love thing."

"No such thing. You love something because it is lovable. There's no value in love that's not deserved."

"Shit, Blake. You're such a prick," Gilbert said. He sipped.

"You think he really is crazy?"

"Sure. A little."

"If Harold did something crazy would you follow?" I asked.

"What? Like walk through the middle of Texas?"

"Something dangerous."

"I think so," he said. "Hell yeah."

"So you think Harold is the Son of God?"

"Fuck no," Gilbert said, his eyebrows popping up. "I'm an atheist." Then his eyebrows slid down until he was frowning. "I don't know."

"You don't have to know." I raised the bottle and handed it over to him.

"I don't have to know." He toasted me and drank.

Gilbert was good. Always good. Years later, as Haroldism bloomed, he attended the first Conference of Haroldistically Sympathetic Churches. The goal was to meet and come to some agreements on the basic tenets of Haroldism. Gilbert Forncrammer succeeded in having himself elected president of the conference. His first and only act as president was to have himself excommunicated.

Gilbert retired to a mountain home in Colorado where he refused to see any visitors, except for the occasional young, female pilgrim. He died a happy man, I have no doubt.

I was lonely that night. The drink only made me more so. I lay down in the living room, listening to the wind peel the paint. The house was howling, as if it were a harmonica that God was blowing away at. The others were all asleep. I got up and left.

I walked a mile and a half to a gas station, was still a little buzzed when I arrived. I found a pay phone and called home. No one answered. I knew no one would. Home had never seemed so far away. I dialed Terry.

"Blake, hey, how are you? Where are you?" It was two in the morning and I was sure I had woken him up, but he sounded thrilled. He asked about Harold, about walking, about everything. I told him a few details. Nothing much.

"Wow. Yes," he said. "Good stuff."

"Terry, have you seen my wife?"

"Jennifer, ah, not recently," he said. "Beth says she's staying with her mother."

"For how long?"

"Well, judging from the height of your lawn, a while."

My mother-in-law. Of course. A woman I did not like and who did not like me.

It was much too late to call, but I called anyway. No one answered. I was grateful. My mother-in-law might have answered and, by that point, I was too cold and too sober to hear her voice. I hung up before the voice-mail beeped.

Another Confession

My house empty, wife and child gone, lawn in disrepair. That's what happens. Leave home—even if you're asked to leave—and everything goes to shit. And I'm walking through a muddy field in the dark to a rotting shack, my newly cleaned feet already a mess.

It was nearly dawn when I got back. A pale blue light filling the east-side rooms. Four bodies asleep in the living room. Shael was awake, in the back room, staring out a thick-glassed window that faced an empty yard surrounded by the remains of a chain-link fence. She turned and smiled as I walked in, then stared out again. I watched her.

"Are you worried?" I asked.

"Yes," she said.

"He wants to die."

"Yes."

I watched again. The room growing lighter.

"Shael," I said, leaning back on the wall. "Do you believe in all this?"

"In all what?" She turned towards me and the early light gave her skin a blue glow.

"About Harold being the Son of God?"

"I love Harold," she said, looking again out to the yard. "There is no one I trust more."

"That's not really an answer."

"I don't know. I don't know what it means to say Messiah or Son of God or Christ."

"So you don't believe?"

"I do believe in Harold," she said. "I just don't know what it means to believe in Harold."

I watched for a moment longer. She rested her head against the window pane. I could see her and her reflection and the point where they touched.

"Do you think he'll die?" I asked.

"I don't know." She said it so softly I could hardly hear. If it hadn't been for the reflection of her moving lips, I might not have known what she said.

I walked over to her. She didn't move. I placed my hands on her shoulders and kissed her neck.

"Don't do that," she said. But I kissed her neck again. She turned to me, her eyes like wet stones.

"Blake," she said, "you would do anything to not be forgiven."

I stepped back. She didn't move her eyes from mine. I turned and left the room.

Shrug

One morning, two days before Christmas, we crossed a bridge over a muddy river. A dark haired woman with narrow shoulders, no older than twenty, stood at the end of the bridge, watching us approach. She didn't walk towards us, just waited, small and still.

"I'm sorry to bother you, but are you Harold Peeks?" she asked when we reached her.

"Yes," Harold said, stopping.

"Please. I need help. I can't hear from my left ear already, and the right one is getting worse. I'm going deaf, and I'm scared, and I've heard you can do things."

Harold smiled. He reached out and put his hands over her ears. Then he removed them. "Your faith has healed you."

"What?" she said. "I didn't catch that."

Harold patted her cheek, shrugged, and walked on.

"Harold," Gilbert said. "Are you just going to leave her?"

"If you can help her, you . . ." Beddy started, but Harold turned.

"There is a peace that lies behind all things," he said. "As you walk today, try to find it."

Tremble

Each day I kneel by the wall in my Mole Hole and sharpen the end of the paintbrush. I whittle and whittle until the point breaks and I have to start again. It snaps every time, all my work is undone, and I find myself smiling.

God has given me this choice. Remain and die a prisoner, or hurt Peter and walk free. I dreamed I had stabbed him in the neck. I dreamed the paintings on the walls cheered, and the books on the shelves clapped their pages. I feel sick.

My hands tremble all the time now.

Christmas

On Christmas Eve we crossed the Colorado River, its waters brown and slow. A rancher near Smithville gave us permission to camp in a meadow on his property. He and his wife, a sweet round woman, brought us out plates of turkey, mashed potatoes, and slices of pumpkin pie. We exchanged kind words and Christmas greetings, and they returned to their home.

We built a campfire under a canopy of sprawling oaks and gathered close. Hardly a word was said. We sat enjoying the light and the crackling until the fire had burned down to coals that you could hear cooling and contracting, pulsing like a slow heart. Harold's eyes were distant, glazed. I wondered if another migraine with its mirrored hole was descending or if the night was simply too quiet. Beddy was reading, his face getting closer and closer to the pages as the light faded. Irma was humming Christmas carols. She hummed them slowly and in a minor key, making each one a lament more than a carol.

"Oh my," she paused and sighed. "I'm missing my daughter something terrible."

"Lo-Ruhamah?" Harold asked.

She nodded. "This is my first Christmas in thirty-five years without her."

"Where'd you find a name like Lo-Ruhamah?" Beddy asked, looking up from his book.

"Well, Bedrick, it's a Bible name," Irma said. "Sure glad she doesn't read the Bible."

"What does it mean?" Gilbert asked.

"You got to read the Bible to find out," Irma said.

"I don't want to read the goddamned Bible."

"Then you won't find out."

"Why would you name your daughter that?" Shael asked.

"You know what it means?" Irma said.

"It's Hebrew," Shael said. "It was in my Bible before it was in yours."

Irma made a little grunt. "I was young and her daddy left me a week before she was born. He didn't want a baby. I didn't want a baby."

"For shit's sake, what's it mean?" Gilbert spat.

"Lo-Ruhamah means 'not loved,'" Irma said.

"You named her that?" Beddy asked.

"But the truth is, once I had her, I loved her more than anything God ever made," Irma said. "More than everything put together with a ribbon around it. Loved her as a baby, loved her as a child, love her all grown up. She even makes housecleaning good when she's with me."

"Yeah. Naming kids is like that," Gilbert said with a nod. "I've got a daughter named Grace. She got all upset when her mother and I split. Hasn't talked to me in twelve years."

Gilbert sucked his teeth for a moment. Beddy closed his book.

"I had a daughter," Shael said quietly.

"I didn't know that. You're a momma?" Irma said.

"No," Shael said. "Past tense. Long time ago. She died."

"Oh," Irma said. "I'm sorry."

"They thought maybe I did it," Shael said, pulling out a cigarette. "I don't know what happened. I was really high. I was really high a lot back then, and she died in her crib. Micah. That was her name." She paused and lit the cigarette. "They arrested me, actually. I was in jail for two nights, charged with neglect, but nothing happened. My mother hired lawyers. The hearing lasted less than two hours, and they told me I was innocent."

"A lot of babies die in their cribs," Irma said.

"I know. That's what the lawyers said." She smiled a little, picked up a stick and poked at the coals. "But I was messed up, so I don't know. Maybe. You know? Maybe I could have helped. They never said I was innocent. They said, 'not guilty.' That's not the same."

"Child," Irma said. She put an arm around Shael and stroked her hair. Harold had leaned back so that his face was in the shadows. Gilbert puckered his lips. He looked embarrassed. Beddy's eyes were wide and glazed, staring into the coals. I watched, not moving, not blinking.

"You're forgiven," I said. I said it so quietly that I wasn't sure anyone would hear. But Shael heard. She looked up at me. She sighed and her forehead wrinkled. Then she released a strange sound, something like a laugh and a sob trying to come out at the same time.

Irma stared at me, as if I'd said something cruel. "Blake," she said and shook her head.

"You too, Irma," I said. "Forgiven."

Neither Beddy nor Gilbert said anything. Beddy glanced at me for a moment and then looked away. Harold stayed back, his face still in the shadows.

There and then, like a snap, I fell in love with Shael and Irma and everyone. They looked like miracles to me, confused and wordless, there in what was left of the firelight. All of us so guilty we could die. All of us alive. I smiled and felt tears in my eyes. I loved my wife. I loved my daughter. I loved Beddy, Gilbert, Harold. I loved my mother and father and any stranger. It was painful. I hurt for Shael and for everyone. I hurt for them like I had hurt for Tammy the day she was born. I looked up and saw the moon and branches in the wind and knew something like God was there and loving. Around me was wind and the sound of Shael's quiet crying, above me was the space between each branch and between the trees and the sky. All these things, like a filling void, like forever. My heart couldn't hold it.

Of course it passed. The instant I tried to look at it, it all vanished. But there was enough in that moment to justify a lifetime.

Blood

I woke up this morning with specks of blood on my pillow. A patch beside my mouth, wet with red spit. I spent the next hour rubbing the blood away before Peter brought my breakfast.

I wonder how my father died. It was sometime during my hiding. I wonder what he thought of me.

I'm sure he died matter-of-factly. "Death is when you stop being alive," he used to say when he'd lose a patient. "That's what people do. It's natural."

He was the kind of doctor who believed comfort was the most important thing he could supply for his patients. Health itself was only valuable if it was accompanied by comfort. He didn't see a long life as a blessing. Once life became uncomfortable, it was better to let it go. He laughed at colleagues who put themselves and their patients through hell to sustain life a year or two longer.

"Our job is not the prevention of death. That's impossible," he'd say. "Our job is improving the quality of life. And the quality of dying."

When something harsh happened like losing a young patient or seeing someone in fierce pain, he refused to believe anything was wrong with the situation. Wrong implied a right, and he believed the universe had no morals. Instead he explained all things as "natural." Children were born, cancer killed, people died. It's natural.

He did not believe life had any meaning. There was pleasure: helping those in need, accomplishing goals, financial stability, family. Days were nice, but amounted to nothing. And he was okay with that. It's natural. Pain existed and you relieved it when you could. But the greatest pains, my father believed, were inevitable. Death, age, loss. I think he took comfort in knowing certain things to be inevitable. No need to complain. No need to waste energy in being frustrated.

He knew a little poem he'd recite that summed up his life philosophy. He used to sing it to me as a child. When I left for college, he wrote it on the inside of a going-away card in which he had also placed a hundred-dollar bill and a picture of him and my mother.

Life is mainly froth and bubble,
Two things stand like stone-
Kindness in another's trouble,
Courage in your own.

Fast

Today, just before lunch, I hid under my desk with my sharpened paintbrush in hand and waited for Peter. An hour passed, then another. Lunch never came. I feel asleep and was curled up like a fetus when Peter finally delivered my dinner.

"What are you doing on the floor?" he asked.

"Praying," I said.

He nodded and turned to leave.

"Wait," I said. "Where was my lunch today?"

"Season of the Fast. Only two meals a day," he said. "Don't you remember?"

Everything Must Go

I remember. Our money ran out halfway through week five. So we begged. Sometimes sitting with an open hand outside a truck stop. Or standing at a traffic light with a sign. It was humiliating. The looks as they handed you a dollar or, more often, the lack of looks.

Worse was the shame. Not for being poor but because I wasn't poor. I still owned a house back in Figwood. I still had a bank account. I was experimenting with a lifestyle that others have forced upon them. And it occurred to me that the dollar some passerby gave me would not be given to someone else, someone with real need.

Often a church gave us sandwiches or a restaurant left us scraps. On New Year's Day, near Manor, Beddy noticed a sealed trash bag in a dumpster behind a Dunkin' Donuts. The bag was stuffed with muffins, bagels, and every color doughnut you could imagine: sprinkles, raspberry, chocolate-chunk, Bavarian cream. Beddy carried the bag over his shoulder, handing out pastries to anyone who'd accept them like some fantastical pastry saint.

"Got your jellies, got your bagels," he sang out. "Who wants a bear claw?"

This was not a fish and loaves miracle. It was the miracle of being homeless in a country so sick with wealth that it throws out food.

But that was already changing.

Soon we were in the outskirts of Austin. Open land and farms turning into suburbs and twenty miles of Home Depot, Wal-Mart, McDonalds, Repeat. Home Depot, Wal-Mart, McDonalds, Repeat. But on a closer look, we saw the parking lots were near empty, gas prices were climbing like acrobats, and every fifth box was closing its doors. We came upon one large electronics store, the same chain I had purchased my flat screen from so many months back. The store's exterior was plastered with liquidation advertisements. "EVERYTHING MUST GO THIS MONTH!" Over a hundred well-dressed people, white resumes in hand, lined up outside the door.

"How many are they hiring?" Beddy asked a young man near the back.

"They didn't say. Ten, maybe."

Gilbert glanced at the line again. "It's just a month long job."

The young man scowled. "You know something better? Point the way."

We moved on, Gilbert rubbing his cheeks and chewing his tongue. "This looks bad," he mumbled at one point. "You could smell fear on those people."

"God's tilling the soil," Irma said. "Must be planning to plant something."

An Introduction to Haroldism

Renouncers

Those who remain in constant pilgrimage are most commonly called Renouncers because they have renounced the world and chosen a path of poverty and prayer. During the skyrocketing unemployment that followed in the wake of the Collapse, many Americans found themselves thrust into poverty against their will. In Renouncing, people found a way to approach their new poverty not as an unfortunate burden but as a chosen act of faith. In those early, turbulent years, it was economic hardships that stole jobs and homes from people. It was Haroldism that allowed them to view their plight as holy.

Renouncing has only grown in popularity. It is estimated that close to 5% of the American population define themselves as Renouncers.

A Renouncer can be recognized by the red stripe drawn or tattooed down the nose. This is referred to as the "Fingerprint of Harold" and signifies the belief that the wearer has been touched and has chosen to leave the responsibilities of work and family in order to seek God.

Most cities in America now feature a Nest or a Renouncer's Field. These parks or campgrounds are reserved for Renouncers.

It has become common to see Renouncers sitting openhanded along city streets in the early mornings. The afternoon is dedicated to public teaching and discussion. The evening is a time of prayer. Often at sunset the low hum of hymns coming from a large city's Nest can be heard for miles around.

There has been an ongoing national debate concerning Renouncers. Many feel that encouraging a lifestyle of begging and vagrancy can only hurt America. Others argue that the Renouncers play an essential role in society. As Josh Erton writes in his book *Road to Roads*, "[Renouncers] are the soul of our future. Their chosen poverty is our culture's penance. They are our walking prayers. In their wanderings we offer our requests and praise. If God smiles upon America, it is in part because we allow these prayers to thrive. So, yes, we must fill their begging hands because the worker is worth his wages."

A more cynical defense was offered by former senator Robert Karyn who said, "There's simply not enough jobs to go around. Thank God they're not trying to get one."

Austin

On the morning of January 6, we arrived in Austin. First just a silver and stone blur to the west, reflecting the pale predawn light. We walked faster, wordless, each of us breathing in the cool air. The growing glow of morning light, the city before, the miles behind, it felt as if the moment was the center of all history. We were the center. We marched through the flat east, gazing at the hills far off to the west, finally touching the city in between. And you could smell the change. Earth stretching its arms in a morning yawn, and the city tapping its feet. Still no words, just slower steps and a new sun behind us coloring everything gold.

Buildings slick and tall, chrome and glass, others brown stone and aged. In the middle, surrounded by taller buildings but still managing to dominate, stood the granite-pink dome of the capitol. From a distance, downtown was clean, structured. The closer we got, the dirtier the city got. But we were dirty too.

Soon people were everywhere, driving cars, cleaning windows, running in state-of-the-art shoes, talking on tiny phones, yelling from roofs. I was walking through a world I was not a part of. People were making money or spending money. It was a community, and I was not a member of the community. The little things were the hardest. Passing a Starbucks, I realized I could not go in. Couldn't sit in the cushy chairs, couldn't browse the espresso machines. I didn't have the money for a cup of coffee, and that was the price of admission. I had become unwelcome. Worse. I had become unseen. The people walking and driving and buying and selling never even saw us. We were ghosts. They moved right by us. The voice on the radio and the picture on the billboard were more real to them.

Strange. To me people had never been so real. The faces overwhelmed me. I had been in crowds before, in traffic jams or elevators. But then a crowd of people was just a crowd, now it was a crowd of people with names and lives. I had never realized that each face had a whole life behind it.

Harold sat on a bench by a bus stop. "Ever hearing, never understanding. Seeing, but not perceiving. Dull ears and closed eyes.

Otherwise they might turn and be healed." He looked at Beddy, "Ask me how long."

"How long?"

"Until the cities are ruins and all the houses empty."

Springs

Our first day in Austin, we found the swimming hole pictured on Beddy's postcard, the one from his bible. It was January, but the sky was clear and the air warm, and the waters of Barton Springs, surrounded by grass slopes and towering oaks, shimmered green in the noon sun. Beddy whooped, stripped to his boxers, and dove right in. No pilgrim walking through the gates of Jerusalem could have been happier. I followed, leaping head first into the waters, the sweet chill touching every part of me, surprising me, waking parts I didn't know were sleeping. I swam deeper and deeper, the waters carrying every trace of the walk's grime from my skin. The quiet of those waters, the clearness of that muted world. Plants waving in slow motion, sunlight stuttering from the surface. At the bottom I ran a hand along the moss-lined limestone floor and finally, feeling my lungs protest, I pushed against the stone and floated back to air.

Gilbert and Irma sat on the side dangling their legs in the water as Beddy and I raced each other across the pool. Harold and Shael walked the circumference of the hole, hand in hand, wading in the shallow waters at the far west end. Eventually, I crawled out, trekked some yards up the hill and lay back in the yielding grass, letting the sun dry my skin and warm me to sleep.

Later, before indulging in the changing rooms' hot showers, all six of us sat on the hillside and talked for an hour. I can't remember a word any of us said, only the buzzing joy that we were together and in Austin.

An Introduction to Haroldism
Feast of the Fast

Perhaps the most popular tradition in the Haroldian calendar is the Feast of the Fast. On this day believers pause from the self-imposed scarcity of the Season of the Fast to prepare an extravagant meal. There are no particulars to the meal, only that every member of the family help in the preparation and that the outcome is truly a feast.

Once the table has been set and the food laid out, the family members exit their home, leaving their front door open. On finding a neighbor's house with an open door, the family enters and enjoys the meal set out, knowing someone is doing the same in their home.

In many parts of the country the meal is followed by street parties and neighborhood carnivals. No holiday better captures Harold's proclamation, "The only way to truly feast is to feed another."

Right as Rain

The next day was gold in the morning, then blue. But in the afternoon a gray-green carpet of clouds rolled in from the west and the air turned cold. Just before five, it started to rain. We tried to stay at a homeless shelter, but they were packed. A volunteer with tired eyes suggested we try another shelter a mile away. "They close their doors at six, so hurry."

A block from the shelter we passed an obese woman kneeling in the rain, picking from a pile of pennies on the sidewalk and dropping them into an oversized jar. Harold stopped and watched her for a moment. Then he knelt beside her and gathered some pennies.

"One penny at a time," the woman said, her eyes never leaving the pile. "One at a time or it won't work."

So Harold started picking up pennies, one by one. Shael knelt down too.

"Harold, it's almost six," Gilbert said. Harold didn't respond. Beddy and Irma joined him on the ground. I helped as well, stooping next to the woman. I could smell her. Wet stink. I could see her thin hair, her red scalp underneath.

"This is my pay. I spilt it. I was in Nam and the Gulf. This is my pay."

"Ah crap," Gilbert said and squatted. "Can't we just scoop them?"

"It won't work that way," she said, still staring at the pile. "You have to do it slowly. Very slowly or it won't work."

The pile wasn't all pennies. There were a lot of buttons and some bottle caps. Too pitiful to stomach. Not just this sad woman, but our charity as well. A pointless act. Nothing gained. And the rain drizzled the whole time.

When we were finished, the woman picked up the jar and squeezed it to her chest.

"Good work, everybody," she said and waddled down the street.

"It's past six," Gilbert said.

"Don't worry," Harold said and started walking.

A block away, I turned and saw the woman dumping the jar on to the sidewalk, shaking out every last coin, button, and bottle cap. The others didn't see and I didn't tell them.

A half hour later we passed a young priest, black shirt and white collar, locking up at a high-arched, downtown church. Shael asked if he could give us a place to stay.

"I'm sorry, I'm afraid we don't have the resources," he said, a little fear in his voice.

"You have a roof."

"I'm sorry," he unlocked the door and stepped back inside. "There's a shelter not too far from here."

We started walking, cutting through alleys and parking lots. It was dark now and cold. But the rain had let up. We turned a corner on to Congress Avenue and there, lit by spotlights, stood the capitol. Less pink at night. More gray.

"Let's see if anyone's home," Harold said and ran across the street and into the grounds.

"Harold, wait," I said, chasing after him.

The grounds were a rolling green lawn filled with oversized oaks also lit up. Harold was standing between a spotlight and an oak. His shadow climbed through the wet branches.

"They left all the lights on," Harold said, making the shadow of a Doberman with his hands. The shadow barked at the capitol. In the drive sat a police car with its parking lights on.

"Here comes Harold," the shadow sang, transforming into a bird. "He's gonna preach up a storm. Gonna speak some truth."

"Come on, Harold. Let's find a place to sleep."

He dropped his hands and turned to me. "I could tear it down," he said. "Every stone."

"The others are waiting."

We made our way south on Congress Avenue passing bars and restaurants. We could hear music being played from blocks away to the east and to the west and on the rooftops above us. On the edge of a strip of water, where Congress Avenue became a bridge, we passed a hotel with large, yellow windows. I could smell food from the connecting restaurant. Warmth and food. Gilbert stopped walking.

"I tell you what," he said. "My treat. Tonight we stay here, get a good bath and a night's rest. Celebrate our arrival."

My whole body smiled at the thought. Beside me Beddy was nodding like a bobble-head doll.

"That'll cost a lot," Irma said.

"Not a worry," Gilbert grinned. "I've got credit." He pulled out his wallet and raised it above his head. We laughed, half for the joke, half out of hope for a warm night.

Harold walked through the rest of us, not smiling. He reached out an open hand to Gilbert. Gilbert looked at Harold's face. He placed his wallet in Harold's hand. For a moment Harold held it on his open palm, as if feeling its weight. Then flung it over the side of the bridge.

I gasped and ran to the edge. I could just see it splash into the reflection of the city. When I turned back around, Harold and the others, even Gilbert, were already walking.

We camped under the overhang of a warehouse. The ground was wet and sleep was hard to come by. The cold creeping into my bones. A man and his son took shelter under the same awning.

"We're okay, aren't we son?" the man kept asking.

"Yeah, Dad," the boy said each time. "Right as rain."

The next morning Beddy woke up at dawn and scrambled off. He came back in an hour with a bag of stale bagels, which we shared with the father and son.

I was grateful for those bagels. Rock hard and dry, but I was so damn pleased. I didn't need to think or make an effort to be grateful, just took a bite and my body thanked God that something like food existed.

It rained again that day. Harold stayed beneath the overhang, leaning against the building and curling into a ball within his red poncho, watching cars pass and puddles form, rubbing his temples with the heels of his hands.

"Harold?" I said. He didn't seem to hear me. "Harold?"

He looked up, pulled from somewhere else.

"We're in Austin," I said. "Now what?"

Half a smile appeared on his lips and he closed his eyes.

We waited, keeping a distance. Hours and hours.

Beddy took a napkin, held it in the rain for a moment and added it to his bible.

"It's getting late," Gilbert said. "Should we try the shelter again?"

"No shelter," Harold said. His first words that day. "Let the others have the shelter."

We stayed in the same spot until a police car pulled up and ordered us to move on. No suggestion as to where to move on to. Just move on.

In the late afternoon we trudged through more of downtown, walking through the condos and cafes on the west side and the east side bars just opening their doors. People on the street hurried past in closed coats and umbrellas, the cold reddening their cheeks and noses. Christmas lights were still strung across Congress Avenue, tinsel on the dismal day. We came upon a crowd, maybe forty, shuffling around the black tinted glass of a corner building. They squeezed near, peering through the windows.

"What's happening?" Shael asked.

"Damn bank won't open. Hasn't opened since last week," a woman said. "They're in there. You can see them, but they won't open the doors or answer the phone or give us our money."

Over their shoulders, I could just see the suited figures moving far behind the glass, pacing from office to office, not risking a glance at the door.

Someone near the front of the crowd banged on the window, shaking the glass. "Hey, we see you!"

Gilbert took a few steps back, almost to the curb. "This is my bank."

Beddy turned. "Do you want to check on your account?"

"No. I mean, I own this bank. Or at least most of it." His face was the color of ash. "I need to make some calls. I need to do something."

"Don't," Harold said.

"Harold, this isn't some Vegas game. It's my business."

"You save it now, the only thing you learn is that it can be saved. And that's a lie. It's dying, like everything else." Harold wiped water from his face, looking around quickly. He jumped onto the hood of a car parked on the street and yelled at the crowd. "Who's surprised? Anyone? Who?" People turned. Harold's face, so corpselike that morning, was now burning. "You're surprised? You thought this, all of this, would last? Everything is going to let you down. Everything. Your banks, your lovers, your children. Not because they don't love you. They're just fuck ups, we're all fuck ups!"

Someone chuckled. Someone else shouted for Harold to shut his mouth. But they might as well have been throwing grass into a hurricane. His eyes met every person standing there, his tone cut through the cold. "Your body will eat itself up and let you die. Your brain will turn soft and throw out all your favorite memories. And God . . . He'll let you down too. I promise. He's going to let babies die and rapists live. He will. He does."

He was breathing hard, white air puffing out. He shook his head slowly.

"There is one thing . . . just one thing. Fainter than a smell you can't catch. One thing that makes any of this worth anything. It's hiding. It's hiding right here now. Love is the closest word, but it doesn't do it justice. But don't look for another word. It will fail as well."

He looked up at the sky and back at the crowd, his voice quiet.

"It's faint. Easy to miss. Not enough to stand up in a courtroom. And that's it, you see. Life is on trial and the evidence is stacked against it. But still, that faint something. That is what I choose. Because of that hint, that splinter of hope, I choose to believe the world is good, being alive is good."

He looked like he might say more. He paused, his mouth moving into the slightest smile. I glanced at the faces watching him, hungry faces. Harold only nodded and stepped down from the car. He put a hand to Gilbert's arm. "Let the dead bury their own," he said quietly. "Say goodbye, Gilbert."

Harold took a step, continuing south. Gilbert didn't move. "I'm sorry, Harold," he said, and Harold turned. "I am sorry, but I can't do that."

Harold's face wrinkled.

Gilbert shook my hand, he hugged Irma and Shael. Beddy squeezed him till he laughed. A thin laugh. Harold only watched. "Goodbye now," Gilbert said and made his way back down the sidewalk. He had a slight limp in his left leg that I hadn't noticed before. I wondered if it was a new ailment, or one I could only see as he was walking away.

Glow and Shadows

When night came, the five of us huddled in an alleyway that smelled like piss. I was hungry, the emptiness in my belly spreading throughout my body. This was walking with the Son of God.

It was dark, but we weren't sleeping. How could we with the rain and Gilbert's absence? We weren't talking either. Each of us had our spot and we kept to it.

Shael was hovering over her Sabbath candles. She shielded the flame from the rain with her hunched shoulders and bent head. Her face glowed and shadows flickered against the alley's walls. I knew those shadows. I closed my eyes and refused to watch them. A wind swept through the alley and spat more water at us. I opened my eyes to see Shael's candles blow out. Her face was as dark as the shadows.

"What the hell is this, Harold?" I asked.

"It's a rainstorm, Blake."

"Why'd you bring us here?"

"So God can find us."

"Can't God can find us in a hotel room? Couldn't he have found us back home?"

"Then you tell me, Blake. Why are you here?"

"Because you're here. You led us here."

"I didn't ask you to come. You invited yourself." He rubbed his eyes. "Wherever you are is exactly where you've walked."

"That's not an answer." I stood up. "I want an answer."

"I'm not here to give you answers." He stood up as well. "Look around you. Feel the stones. Stop being so afraid. You're afraid of everything."

"How can you say that? How can you? I'm here. I walked."

"You came because you were afraid of being left out. Fear decides everything for you."

The rain let up a little and Shael relit her candles. Again the glow and shadows filled the space between us.

"Do you see?" he asked, looking at all of us. "You already know this story. I don't have much time."

"What does that mean?" Beddy asked.

"You know what it means," I said. "He wants to die."

"Beddy, don't worry. I'm following God," Harold said, pressing his forehead.

"You think God wants you to die?" Beddy asked.

"I don't know," Harold said. "I have no idea."

Another gust of wind and the candles went out again. No one spoke. I sat back down. So did Harold. For a while, no one said a word.

"Blake." He turned and looked at me, water falling from his hair. "Call your wife."

I thought to ask, but I didn't. I went to find a pay phone and do as I was told.

I called my mother-in-law collect, waiting for an answering machine to not accept the charges. But instead my daughter's voice answered.

"Tammy?"

"Hi, Daddy." Her voice was softer. No anger in it. That scared me. "Mom is sick."

"Can I talk to her?"

"No, Dad, she's real sick," she said. "She's in the hospital."

That's how the walk ended for me. I had my daughter order me a ticket for a midnight bus. Harold offered to walk me to the bus station.

I said goodbye to the others in that alleyway. Shael hugged me and whispered goodbye into my ear. I couldn't speak. I just nodded. Beddy teared up, said he'd see me soon. It wasn't true. This was a final goodbye for us, and somehow I knew it. I could feel the ending. Dear God, I wanted to stay in that alley. Stay with those wet fools. Leaving was ripping me. Irma was last to say goodbye, her hug tight, fierce as a mother's. I could smell her. My throat felt full. She let go, touched my face with the palm of her hand. I turned and walked away with Harold by my side.

Harold's Confession

The rain was strange that night, quieting the world. The streetlights and headlights were mellowed by the drizzle, and on the emptier streets the soft splashes of our steps were the only sounds. Harold and I headed towards the bus station some miles away. Before long the rain eased up, only an occasional drop falling. Already I was feeling a lonely so thick it ached in my muscles. Hidden inside the lonely was a panic, a little beast waiting, urging me on—she's sick! Run! Run!—wanting me alone so it could pounce. But for now, the quiet of the night and the rhythm of our steps kept it at bay.

We walked. I wanted Harold to say I would be okay, or insult me, or something. But for a mile or more he said nothing. We were out of downtown before long, walking through quieter streets lined with small old houses. Warm yellow light coming from the windows. Homes, people's homes. Inside, I imagined families, children, maybe having a meal, maybe sleeping.

After two miles or so Harold spoke.

"Phil. He was my best chance," he said. "I lived in three countries before I turned six. California, England, Argentina, and then to Texas. My father was in oil. He was a greedy, cold man. He died in Texas and we stopped moving." His tone was one I had never heard from Harold. It was hard to hear. His voice was clear, but very quiet. It was as if he wasn't talking to me, he was just talking. "My mother remarried a chemistry teacher. Phil. He was kind, always kind, and he loved my mother dearly. He was also terribly boring. At the time, all I saw was boring. In all the years we shared a house, I never called him dad. Just Phil. One time, just once, he tried calling me son. It was high school graduation, just after the ceremony. Everyone was standing around the high school gym. 'I'm proud of you, son.' He said it fast. I could tell he had rehearsed it. Maybe practiced in a mirror. My mom was holding his arm and smiling. It was embarrassing. I pretended I hadn't heard and ran off with some friends."

Harold was quiet for a moment. I was afraid to say anything. Afraid I would break this mood.

"It would have been good to be Phil's son. And he would have liked to be my father, I know. But neither one of us could believe it. We both believed a greedy dead man was my father. That's what I'd been told.

Didn't even know I had a choice. Even my mother couldn't believe that Phil could take that role. So much of those years could have been better, but we didn't know how to believe it."

We reached the bus station, but Harold kept walking and although I felt the panic urging me home, I didn't dare interrupt.

"All the things I just believed. Just did. Never imagined anything more than I was given. Even my fantasies were just scenes from movies or books. But at that company banquet last year . . . remember?"

I nodded.

"The next day was my birthday. Did you know that?"

"No," I said.

"No one did. But it was. While sitting there, during the first of the speeches, I could feel one of my headaches coming on. I tried to focus on my water glass. Sometimes that helps. But the pain came and that growing void. I couldn't hear the speech or eat my food. The headaches are like that. I can't stomach noise or people. So I crawl into my head, pull the curtains, and lock the door. That's what I was doing that night. I stayed in my head. Just me and my thoughts. I thought, 'What if I'm actually a relative of Hitler and never knew it?' and 'What if I'm the reincarnation of Da Vinci?' Just a game, you see. Then I thought, 'What if I'm the Son of God? God's favorite. What if I believed it?' It was a question. A game. But as soon as the question popped in my head, I knew it was true. Immediately I knew I was the Son of God and the headache was gone. Just like that. Then the vice president called my name and held out that plaque. The whole world seemed so silly and beautiful. That's how it happened."

Dark rainbows floated in the puddles. They swirled as we stepped. A car passed, its high-beams blinding me for a moment.

"There was no voice? No flash?" I asked.

"It was like a voice." He paused for a moment, sniffed the air. "Maybe it was a sort of voice. The voice said, 'Jump,' and I jumped. I'm midair now. I'm falling. I still don't know if God is going to catch me, and sometimes I'm sure He won't. Sometimes I'm sure no one is there. But, wow, the falling. That's the point. God be praised. If it's a lie, what a wonderful lie."

"You'd live for a lie?"

"What was I living for before? Really? If it's a lie that God is my father and calls my name, I choose to believe it. And believing it is as close as I've ever been to truth."

"Yeah, but if it's not real . . ."

"I tell you, Blake, even if it isn't real, He is still the biggest thing in my life. He is closer to me than I am to me. I disappear. It's not just that I see God, it's that I see nothing but God."

"What if it's all just another migraine, Harold?"

"No. Not like that. The woman with the jar of pennies, the river, Shael. Like the rain on that tree, each drop catching light. Same light, different drops. I see that light. And when the drops dry, the light will be all there is. There is love, Blake. There is love enough to burn everything away."

We had walked around in a circle and now we were again heading toward the bus station.

"What will you do now, Harold?"

"Preach," he said. "I'm going to stand up on walls and tell them about that love. I'm going to feed them mouthfuls of God. Some are waiting. Some will choke because they can't remember how to swallow. Some will hate every word I say."

"You really do want to die, don't you?"

"Who ever heard of a messiah growing old?"

We walked into the station. It was bright. All the quiet was lost. I collected my ticket and we sat in plastic chairs waiting.

"Harold," I said. "I'm afraid."

"I know. Listen to it like you listened to the pain while walking. Don't feed it," he said. "There are some hard things coming your way. My way too."

The bus pulled up outside, a loud, grumbling thing.

"Blake, do you remember Steven? The one who ran the music store?" Harold asked. "Give him this if you see him." He handed me a folded piece of paper. "I never got a chance."

"What does it say?" I asked as I slipped the note into my pocket.

"That's none of your concern, Blake."

I reached out my hand and shook Harold's.

"I'm glad you came," he said. "You're a good friend. And we'll see each other again."

I started to climb aboard the bus but turned and asked Harold one last question.

"Austin isn't really holy, is it?"

"Of course it is." He smiled. "Holy travel makes a holy destination."

For a moment, standing on the steps of the bus, I saw my chance. I could be what he was. I could be a son. The idea was like a bubble in my heart. But I walked on, the doors closed, and the bubble burst.

Bus

I sat by the window and let my head bounce against the glass as the bus rumbled east. It was cold outside so the heater pumped hot, thick, sweat-scented air. Ten minutes from the city limit of Austin, the panic squeezed. I felt sick, angry at every person on that bus. Two days earlier I had been lying under live oaks with the others, watching the green against the blue and believing I could smell God on my hands. I had loved everyone, but this was the morning after. No affection, no gratitude for the people sharing this trip. Their loud, ignorant conversations. Their racist slurs. The yelled threats aimed at their children. For God so loved the world? Maybe God should take a night ride across Texas on a Greyhound bus.

That bus was the world. Too small for the crowd, the floors sticky with soft drinks and spit, filled with pointless words, and the driver just driving, hardly aware of his passengers. Now and then he piped through on the intercom, but it was a blown system filled with static. So, just like with God, we couldn't understand a word.

"He said the next stop was Gidder."

"No he didn't. He said Bridder."

"Bullshit."

Next would come a holy war.

I wanted off. But I wouldn't get off. I only fell asleep.

The road thumped and thumped and thumped beneath me. I rolled around in a groggy, restless sleep. My dreams were smeared with crying babies and the stink of people. Every so often the bus stopped and new bodies pushed their way in. Hours passed, and I felt no closer to Houston. The night didn't want to end. People. The couple fighting in a language I couldn't recognize, an old man talking to himself in the very back of the bus, the hungry-looking teenage girl sitting next to me and whispering in my ear, "I'll suck you for fifty dollars." When I shook my head, she said she was sorry and disappeared. The squealing laughter from somewhere else, the drone of the engine, the large man leaning over me to try and see shooting stars. "The news said there'd be hundreds of 'em," he said. "Too many to even see." The woman telling her daughter she had no more diapers for the baby. All the seats were full, the windows were dark, and the bus rocked back and forth. Why weren't you on that bus, Harold?

Slowly the sky went from black to blue, and Houston lay before us.

Sorry Sight

It wasn't until I got off the bus that I remembered Harold's note for Steven. I pulled it out, uncrinkled the paper, and read the words.

Who said you'd like what you see?

Tomorrow I stab Peter and leave this place.

The Damage I Did to Peter

I woke this morning with courage. I cleaned the basement. I sat on my cot and waited with my sharpened brush behind my back. He was late. For the first time. I thought perhaps he wouldn't come and I'd have to die. It wasn't a bad thought. What will I gain by being free? Nothing but being free. But that's something, isn't it?

The lock turned and I put my doubts away, like a child with his toys. Peter came in with a tray.

"Good evening," I said. He nodded slowly. I wouldn't jump while he was looking. I waited. His steps were slow. Perhaps he was distracted. Good, I thought. Easier that way. Finally, he turned his back to place down the tray. I jumped. In my mind's plan, I landed on his back like a monkey, wrapped one arm around his head and stabbed his neck with the other.

But the reality of what happened was disappointingly different. My jump was pitiful, almost a falling forward. I landed low, wrapping my arms around his chest, more like a baby chimp. Peter yelled. Well, not quite a yell. More a groan of annoyance. The tray fell, my dinner and a stack of papers scattered. I clung tight with one arm as Peter twisted around. With the other, I reached up as high as I could and stabbed. I gave it all the strength I had. I prepared myself for the sensation of skin puncturing. Readied myself to keep pushing the point further in. But I hit something hard and the brush snapped.

"Ow!" Peter said, as if a small wasp had stung him. With a flick of his arms, he threw me off and I fell. The ground knocked the air out of me, and my head smacked against the leg of the desk. The paintbrush was protruding from the shoulder of his sweater. There was no blood.

Peter looked down at me, pulling the stick out and rubbing his collar bone. Still no blood. Maybe he'll bruise.

"I didn't think you'd do it." His voice was angry, like a disappointed parent. "I read it: 'I will stab him in the neck' over and over, but I didn't believe you'd have the nerve."

"You . . . read . . ." I still didn't have the breath.

"Did you think I wouldn't? You left them out. It was easy to take." He groaned and rubbed a little more. "You bastard."

My pants were wet. At first I thought I had soiled myself, but it was the soup Peter had been carrying. I was sitting in soup and yellow pages, still gasping for air. I tried to gather the pages—my pages—tried to lift them from the soup, but they fell apart in my hands.

Peter stared. I stopped and stared back. His eyes were strange, not gray, not cold. For an instant, I was sure he would kill me.

"Ha!" he yelled. He stuck the pointed stick at me, not as a weapon, more like a magic wand. "It's true," he said, and smiled. A real Beddy smile. I found it more frightening than the anger. "It's all true. Harold and 4 and salvation and all of it. And you believe it too. That's what you're confessing."

"You had no right to read these," I said, a wad of wet paper in my fist.

"Oh yeah, and you have the right to stab me." He was smirking, more boyish than I'd ever seen him. "Your writing is what got me. I hate that *Harold Be Thy Name* movie. Never believed a scene. But you. I believe your stuff. I mean, hell, you shot him and still believe in him. Oh, God. I really get it!"

"No," I said.

"And here's the punch. I forgive you. For stabbing me, for everything. I completely forgive you. In fact, here's your stick back." He knelt down, opened my fist, and put the handle on top of the wet pulp. "Nice touch, by the way. A paintbrush on one end, a dagger on the other. Creation and destruction all in one." He winked. He actually winked! He stood up and put his hands on his waist. "See, I gave to the one who tried to kill me. I just gave to God. How about that?" He shook his head. "I see it now. Wow. This feels really different. Really good. Thank you." Then he quickly knelt again and pushed his face close to mine. His voice went quiet and serious. "What is it you want, Mr. Waterson? Do you want to escape? I can give you that too."

"I want to go to bed."

He nodded. Without another word he helped me dry off, helped me undress, helped me to my cot. He said nothing, but occasionally laughed a little, as if remembering a joke he'd heard earlier that day.

Questions

Question I asked Harold:

"What is God like?"

Harold's answer:

"Close your eyes," he said. I did. I waited. And waited. I opened my eyes. He had walked away.

BOOK III

Home

Terry met me at the bus stop and drove me home, informing me that my daughter was at her grandmother's and I'd see her at the hospital. The lawn was an uneven patchwork of weeds. Unrolled newspapers lay scattered along the driveway. Inside, the house smelled stale, that subtle odor of an unoccupied home. I fell asleep on the living room couch.

Later Terry drove me to the hospital for visiting hours. Tammy met me in the waiting room looking older, her eyes all grown-up. I hugged her and she cried. My mother-in-law hid herself behind a magazine, but I had nothing I could say to her anyway. Then I saw my wife.

She was dying. I knew it the moment I saw her lying in that clean, narrow hospital bed. She was asleep, taking in loud gasps and looking thirty pounds smaller. Her hair was thin, the color of dead grass. Her skin, yellow.

"Jennifer?" I said. She opened her eyes and smiled.

"You look different," she said. It hadn't occurred to me, but my hair had grown, and I, too, had lost weight.

"Yeah, I guess I do."

"I bet I look different."

"You look beautiful," I said.

"I don't feel it." She smiled. "It was there for a while. In my ovaries, just growing and spreading, and I didn't even know."

I nodded and squeezed her hand. She nodded too. Soon she closed her eyes and seemed asleep. I watched her face. There was no peace in her expression. Just discomfort. I rose to leave.

"We have to talk about Tammy," she said without opening her eyes. "You need to think about what's best."

"There's plenty of time," I said.

"That's not true."

I sat back down and put my hand to her cheek. She leaned her face into my palm and rested. I stayed until she was sleeping.

In the waiting room, I asked to borrow Terry's car. He gave me the keys without question or hesitation. I told Tammy I was going for help.

"Dad, there's no where to go."

I told her not to worry. I'd be back very soon and everything was going to be all right.

"Please don't leave, Dad."

I drove out of Houston on the same road I had ridden in on that morning. It took half the time to trace my path. I passed signs for towns we walked through, rivers we had crossed. Over forty days of walking in three hours of driving. My head was heavy with exhaustion, but I didn't dare to stop. By dusk I was standing in the alleyway where I had last been with the others. They were gone, so I drove on. I looked down other alleyways, public parks, shelters. I prayed as I drove and rolled down the window screaming out Harold's name. I found bums and college students and hookers and cops and kids and trash and piss and vomit but no Harold. So I drove on, checking golf courses and open fields. More alleys and abandoned buildings.

Morning birds were beginning to shriek when I found them under a bridge on the south part of town. I tiptoed through the sleeping bodies. First I found Shael. Then Harold sleeping under his poncho. I shook him and whispered his name until he looked fully awake.

"Okay, Harold, I believe in you. Completely believe. I know who you are. You're the Messiah or the Christ or whatever. Is that it? Is that what you want? Now save her."

"I won't," he said.

"Yes, you will. She's sick. I've seen her. She is sick."

"She is supposed to be sick."

"You pick and choose, you bastard. You pick and choose." I wasn't whispering anymore and I saw Shael's eyes blink open.

"She is going to die," he said. And I saw pity in his face. Worthless, boneless pity. I grabbed his shirt and lifted him towards me.

"That's not fair, Harold."

"You should thank God he isn't fair," he said without flinching.

"Shut up!" I pushed him away from me. "What if it was Shael, Harold? What would you do then?"

Harold looked over at Shael who was watching us with wide eyes.

"I don't know," he said.

"Then help Jennifer."

"No, Blake."

"I lied. I don't believe in you."

"Yes, you do," he said. "Now go be with your wife."

I drove. A slow drive. My body and head drained. Everything but my eyes was asleep. Mindless and soulless. In all those hours only one thought seeped through. I loved my wife after all. The driving, the fear, were evidence. It's unforgivable that I had to go so far to understand it.

It was mid-morning when I reached my house. I gathered the old newspapers from the driveway and emptied a stuffed mailbox of unpaid bills, junk mail, and a box of business cards I'd ordered before I quit Promit. I carried them inside, slumped up the stairs to a bare bed, and slept.

Six hours later I woke up and went down to the kitchen to see if there was anything to eat. I hadn't eaten since the stale bagels, and my stomach was cramping. I checked the pantry and found two cans of corn and some olives. As the corn heated on the stove, I sat down at the kitchen table popping olives into my mouth.

God's Missing Leg

The next day my wife didn't open her eyes. Terry was waiting for me in the hospital lobby.

"I've got something to show you," he said. "It might cheer you up a little."

He drove me to his house. I didn't speak. I just watched Figwood pass on the other side of his tinted windows. I smiled a little. *Hello, little town,* I thought. *Silly little town.*

"I want to show you what I've been doing while you were gone," Terry said. He led me upstairs to his office, a dark room lit primarily by his computer screen. He pulled up an extra chair and we both sat in front of the computer. He pressed a button on the keyboard and up came www.haroldpeeks.com.

"Oh my God," I mumbled.

"Pretty cool, huh?" he nodded at the screen, his red hair bouncing. "It's been up about a month, but I keep making improvements. I just added these graphics. I've only got this one picture of Harold. You didn't take a camera with you, did you?"

The picture was dark and difficult to make out. I could recognize Harold's room at the old folks home. It was Terry and Harold standing together, both smiling like drunks. It looked as if Terry had extended his arm and taken the picture himself.

"Does Harold know about this?"

"Not yet. I can't wait to show him. We get hundreds of emails every day asking how to contact him. I've been taking sick days to answer them all," he said. Terry rubbed his hands and his knee bounced as he talked.

"You said 'we.'"

"Sure, I mean the community. The people who use this page. Over three thousand hits a day. Check out this forum. People discuss Harold's ideas or write in testimonials. There're people all over. Houston and out west. All these miracles that people have seen. Amazing stuff. He cured someone's cancer, saved a baby with third-degree burns, healed someone's diabetes. That's a sweet lady, the diabetes lady. Writes me every day and thanks me for the page." Terry slapped his knees and jumped to his feet. "Let's have some coffee!" He started scooping grounds into a tiny coffeemaker sitting on a file cabinet. I read the forum comments.

"This guy says Harold founded a Young Republicans group at the University of Nebraska?"

"Yeah, that's pretty cool," he said from behind me. "He knew him in college."

"You think Harold is a Republican?"

"It's not about parties, Blake. It's about winning America back. Everyone is welcome."

"Terry," I said, rubbing my forehead. "How do you know these folks aren't just crazy or lying?"

"Good question, Blake. I've got a simple rule. If it sounds like Harold, then I let it stay. Otherwise I take it down. You're right, there's some crazy stuff out there. Some guy in Santa Fe says Harold is an official member of his Mosque. I saw that and thought, 'Ah, no, thank you,' and took it down."

The coffeemaker sputtered and Terry shook it.

"There's the lesbians in Dallas who claim to have had an orgy with Harold. One person swears they saw him levitating over Lake Jackson. A while back someone wrote in this story about Harold standing up in their church and yelling, 'I'm God's cock! I'm God's cock!'" Terry shook his head and poured the coffee. "I took them all down."

"That last one is true," I said.

"Oh, I doubt it," he said and handed me a cup. "Check this out." He sat down and clicked on a star-shaped icon. The screen went black. Silver colored text faded.

Like a thief in the night . . .

Black again. Then more words.

Sign up for Harold's Summer Conference.

"I got some help from some friends at church. We've started meeting. Planning."

"Planning for what?"

"The conference. The future, Blake. Harold is just the beginning. This is big. We've been writing articles, sending them out. Things are changing. One woman, Cynthia Bock, she was a religious studies minor at Baylor and she thinks, just an idea, but she thinks maybe Harold is like another part of the trinity, making it a foursome. Which, to me anyway, makes perfect sense. I mean, think about it. And I have.

Jesus was a carpenter. I bet he never built a table with three legs. Ha! Four legs make a table, makes a chair. Four walls make a house, four gospels make a New Testament, four seasons in the year. Harold is the final season, God's missing leg. Pretty wild, huh? We're thinking about making buttons and bumper stickers with the number four on them. Just that. Get a buzz going. Get people asking, 'Hey, what's the four for?'" Each time Terry said "four," he raised four fingers in the air. "See? Double meaning. Is there anything worth living *four*? Is there such a thing as *four*-giveness? We're *four* Harold. Pretty good, huh?"

"Did Harold tell you these things?"

"Harold wants us to think for ourselves. He just gives clues. It's up to us to really dive in and work it out. That's what I've been doing. Now I can help others. And others can help me, I'm sure. I don't mind that."

More phrases faded in and out. Bible verses, personal testimonials, and some quotes attributed to Harold.

This is what language is for.

"Remember that, Blake?" Terry asked me, his eyes reflecting the shine of the screen. "At your house. The night you killed Pickles."

"I didn't kill Pickles."

"Oh, I just presumed you had."

"No, for God's sake."

"Oh."

"Is that on your web page?"

"It can be removed."

"I need to go home, Terry." I stood up.

"This is big, Blake," Terry said, looking up at me from his chair. "Harold is a catalyst. This movement is bigger than just one man. But I'm looking forward to Harold coming home. I've been invited to do a few speaking engagements. I'd love to bring him along. You know, at first when he said I couldn't go with y'all I was upset. I was hurt, even. But now I understand. I had another job. Another way to follow. I had to make this web page, answer these emails, spread the word. Big things. God things. And you and I are right in the middle of it. I know what I was made *four*. I know what I'm living *four*. I know what we should be planning *four*. America is blessed again, Blake. Right now. I've already signed you in, by the way. You're on the list. You should be getting weekly emails. Okay, you've gotta go, okay, I'll see you later. Okay. I'll be praying for Jennifer. Okay."

What Harold Wanted

If Harold hadn't died, there would be no Haroldism. He could never have been so popular while alive. We like our heroes dead, less chance of disappointing us. Van Gogh, JFK, Janis Joplin, James Dean. Let them promise. Let them die. Messiahs, politicians, and superstars.

And who knows what he would have said, what he would have done, had he lived much longer. He was unstable, especially towards the end. He could never live up to his own promise. Who can?

Peter is Planning

Peter has a plan. He grins at me, whispers assurances that he's "working on it." Sometimes he flashes me four fingers.

My Wife Died

Jennifer died on January 30, three weeks after my return home It was hot. I remember that. Too hot for winter. People in Figwood were strolling around stubbornly wearing sweaters and coats, doing their best to pretend that things were not as they were.

I was not there when Jennifer died. They called me at home and said to come quickly. By the time I had arrived, she was gone. The doctor shook my hand like a politician. "She passed away a few minutes ago."

Tammy and my mother-in-law joined me moments later, and the doctor offered to let us see her. Tammy refused, so my mother-in-law and I left her in the waiting room. Jennifer was in the bed. I touched her. Her face felt soft and warm.

I spoke her name once and touched her hair. At the time, I remember trying to be angry that the hospital hadn't called me earlier so I could have been there for her last breath. But the truth is I was relieved. I wouldn't have known what to say, what to do. So I wasn't there when she died, which is fitting. I was hardly there when she lived.

Through all of this, Jennifer's mother stood behind me breathing out quiet moans like a child after a tantrum. I got up to leave and she followed.

Tammy stood waiting outside. When I came out, I put my arms around her and kissed her forehead. She walked with me and moved towards my car. My mother-in-law attempted to object, saying Tammy was coming home with her, but it was too hot and too sad to argue. So Tammy left with me.

I was her father again. I had no idea what to do or who to be. Everything I thought I had learned from Harold was gone. We drove through the slow streets past half-crowds and non-smiles. At home we tramped through rooms like ghosts. I made coffee and Tammy went to sleep in her room. Later I ordered pizza for dinner. It sat in front of us untouched for half an hour.

"Dad," Tammy asked. "What was it like when she died? Did the doctor say anything?"

"They gave her painkillers," I told her. "She didn't feel a thing."

Tammy might have hated me before, and she might hate me now, but for those three days she had no energy for hate and we were father and daughter.

Sometimes we talked. I told her stories about the day she was born. She told me about a boy at school she liked. I told her things that Beddy had done that made her laugh. Often we didn't talk at all. We shared the house in silence. Others came by with a casserole or a card, wanting a piece of our grief in exchange, but we wouldn't let them have any. They could say they were sorry, and then they had to leave.

The funeral was February 2, Groundhog Day. Tammy and I walked into the church together with Jennifer's mother immediately behind us, her high heels clicking against the church tiles like the firing of an empty cartridge.

All of our friends squeezed in with their tailored black suits and dresses. All decked out for a good long cry. The reverend melodically sang my wife's praise. "Let me tell you of her life . . ."

Let *me* tell you of her life. Because I do still remember. Camping in the Redwoods, making love in a two-person tent. Getting drunk on the cheap wine we smuggled into the movie theater. The day the flowers from our wedding died and she cried. The day her father died and she cried even more. I can see her giving birth to Tammy. Her eyes wide with wonder and fear. Then we grew up and I got lost in work and she got lost at home and I stopped loving her and she left me and then she died.

The sermon was about Lazarus dying. Jesus showing up three days late and then weeping. "Move the stone," Jesus said and out stumbles the corpse. "Jesus is our hope," the reverend proclaimed. "He is our resurrection."

I imagined Jesus arriving at my wife's tomb and yelling for her to come out. She'd take a look at her moldy grave clothes, a quick whiff of the embalming fluid, and yell back, "I can't go out looking like this." The thought made me smile, and I missed her so much my head hurt.

We walked to the grave and they placed the box in the ground. It was a varnished honey-oak coffin that her mother had picked out. The side had brass handles and imitation ivory inlays. My wife was inside.

People came back to the house and ate tiny sandwiches and spoke in quiet tones and acted embarrassed that all this had happened. Tammy and I stood by the wall and nodded thanks as face after face told us how sorry they were.

My parents, the good doctor and his wife, were there. They patted my shoulder and hugged Tammy. "Hell of a killer, cancer. Just grows and kills," my father said.

At one point during the afternoon I felt a hand on my back. I looked over my shoulder and saw Terry with his eyes closed and his lips moving.

"Are you praying for me?" I asked.

He opened his eyes. "A little," he said.

"Well, don't."

"Sorry." He stepped away and I noticed the small button on his lapel with a bold "4" typed on it. A few of the other guests had similar buttons.

I moved to a corner of the living room and watched the crowd. My house was filled with uncles and aunts and neighbors and tennis partners and fellow PTA members and anyone else who was hungry for tiny sandwiches and a thick slice of mourning. But all of these people were strangers and I wanted them to leave.

Finally they started to slip away. My mother-in-law took me aside as the crowd thinned out and told me I might have shaved for her daughter's funeral. Then, as I palmed my stubble, she told me I was in no condition to care for a child so she would be taking Tammy home with her.

When I opened my mouth to object, my voice sounded hoarse and childish. I looked at my hands. They were trembling.

"But I would like her to stay here."

"That's not enough of a reason to make a child live like this, Blake. Besides, all her clothes are already at my house."

"Is this what Tammy wants?"

"Of course it is. But she's too sweet a girl to let you know that." She looked around to make sure she wasn't overheard and whispered, "You know that Jennifer would agree. She did leave you."

And that was that. Goodbye, Tammy. Goody goody bye bye.

Later I sat alone at the dinner table eating the last of the tiny sandwiches. The sun set and the room grew darker, but I had no reason to turn on any light. I leaned back and watched the world grow black and waited for the shadows. But that night there were no shadows.

I had lost my wife, my daughter was gone, I had no job, no television, no next step . . . we thank you God for the gifts you bring.

I Know

My wife won't visit the Mole Hole. She peeks in from the vent, but, no matter how much I beg, she refuses to come any closer.

Hermit

I lived alone for the next six weeks. My world was a rotten floor—I never knew if my next step would break through the boards and send me spiraling. That silence. That abyss. Not forward from silence or backward from silence, but downward into silence. The moments between lying down and falling asleep were the edge of a void. I could feel that cold blackness pulling me in.

I have heard it said that a mourning spouse will be reminded of the lost love by the most trivial souvenir of their life together. A photo, a candlestick, or a bedside table will bring back too many memories. This didn't happen to me. The furniture, the decorations, her clothes were all lies. They were masks and make-up. They begged to be mistaken for my wife. Maybe she would have joined their begging, but they were not her. I grew tired of their high-pitched squealing, so I burned them.

My first bonfire was set up in the backyard. It was just a few clothes and the kitchen stools. But a policeman came by and told me I wasn't allowed to have a bonfire without a permit. So I put the fire out and built another one inside. I used the couch. I piled on her old summer dresses and doused it with her perfume. I recognized the smell, and it whispered, "I am her." But it wasn't. So without hesitation I took her hairspray and aimed the spray through a lighter's flame. The fire was huge, the flames licking the ceiling. The smell of her skin still clung to the bed sheets, they burned too. I added shoes and scarves and fashion magazines—each protesting that although the others had been imposters, it really was her. I burned them all and opened the windows so that not even the smoke would stay.

I sat beside the fire watching the colors change in the twisting flames. The fire alarm went off, and I added it to the pile. Even with the windows open the room was full of smoke and the smell of melting plastic. The smoke was down in me. It was crawling through my eyes. The sand was now smoke, moving fast and drowning me all the same. And through the smoke, on the far side of the fire, I could see Harold standing. I could see him seeing me. I stood up, squinting through the flames and said his name aloud. And from where he was an invisible fist slammed into my chest and I was on my back. Something was roaring.

Water exploded into my fire. I darted out the back door and hid in the yard as the scuffed helmets and heavy jackets dragged a hose through my home, shot water with the force of a cannon, smashed lamps and windows. I watched with the fascination of a child.

Then they left and I returned to the house. Wet black ash covered the living room and the resin of smoke coated my brain. Now I could remember her. I sat still and let my mind see her. No things, no moments, not even her words. Just her in my head. I remembered until I was too tired to remember anymore.

I gathered a beach towel and a damp pillow and walked to the corner of the backyard. I asked the kittens if they'd mind the company. I took their silence as approval and slept by their tiny graves. Another night in another graveyard.

After the fire came boredom. It had been less than a month since I had sat beneath a sky so blue it sang, and I had believed I would never, could never, be bored again. So much to see and so much to think. But boredom came. Dear God, save us from boredom. It is our worst creation.

What now? What now? What now? What now?

Some days I'd turn on the shower but not get in. I'd stand there naked and dirty only allowing the steam to touch me. Then they turned off the water because no one had paid the bill. The electricity and phone went too. The house had never been so quiet. No whizzing and whirring, no moving air. At night it was dark. Sometimes it was cold.

Terry came by, but I wouldn't answer the door. He'd leave food on the front step. Fast food, greasy and sweet. I never acknowledged his gifts beyond taking them. I knew nothing about what was happening outside my walls. I supposed Harold was dead, or soon would be. That was his plan.

Once my father visited, a four-hour drive for him. I watched him knocking from the window in Tammy's room, but I didn't let him in. After twenty minutes, he turned back to his sedan, climbed in, and drove away. That was the last time I saw him.

The roaches came. Clicking and scuttling. They abandoned the walls and cupboards and ran fearlessly throughout the house. They scurried over my body when I slept and over my feet as I paced. My home had never been so alive.

I thought to die. I found my old handgun in the back of the closet. Something I'd bought a decade before for "home protection" and had never fired. But I had bullets. I loaded the gun and put the barrel to my forehead. I pressed hard. Rested a finger on the trigger. I pushed harder, bruising my skin, trying to push the bullet into my brain. But I couldn't pull the trigger. Couldn't do it. Not wanting to live is not as strong as wanting to die. Suicide takes courage, motivation. I had neither, so I lived by default. All I had managed to do was give myself a little red circle on my forehead like an empty third eye.

Went All Names

One morning, naked on the mattress I had shared with Jennifer, I woke to the sound of knocking. I let it go. Then came a key turn and the squeaking of the front door. I wrapped a blanket around me and crept halfway down the stairs. There in the living room was my mother-in-law staring at the charred couch.

"Hello," I said.

"Dear God," she jumped, giving me the most pleasure I'd had in weeks.

"How are you?"

"Better than you. What the hell happened here, Blake?"

"I'm fine, thanks. Can I get you something?"

"Why is it so cold in here?" She flipped a switch on the wall and then another and then one more and each time nothing happened. "Your power is out!"

"Yeah."

"And did you know your phone is disconnected?"

"Yes."

"How can you live like this?"

"Actually the majority of humans throughout history have lived like this."

"We're in the midst of a national crisis and you're doing nothing. Par for the course, Blake. Really."

I stared.

"I came to get some of Jennifer's things," she said.

"Good luck."

I sat in my leather recliner with nothing on except my blanket, watching her scoop up frames, blenders, and tiny porcelain statues, like a gerbil scurrying around its cage, gathering pellets from the cedar chips.

"Where's the rest of her clothes?" she paused to ask.

"Fire."

"Her photo albums?"

"Fire."

"Did you burn them?"

"Nope. The fire did."

She grunted and continued her scavenging.

"How's Tammy?" I asked as she tore past with a box of cookbooks.

"Tammy is just fine, all things considered."

"Please tell her I love her."

"Of course," she said, but I knew she wouldn't.

She worked without ceasing for an hour and then left. I missed her as soon as she closed the door. I stayed in the chair for the next hour, and that hour smeared itself into several hours and finally an afternoon. I could hear cars passing, dogs barking, a school bus stopping—all muffled. When the sun had gone and it was dark, I grabbed my box of business cards and walked out to the backyard.

The lawn was wild. Grass to my shins. The pool was even stranger. It had come to life over the months, changing from dead blue to a brownish green. For years I had kept it dead by adding chemicals and scrubbing the life away. Left alone, it thrived. A new smell, earth and mold. It was the smell I had always associated with death, but in truth it's the stench of life. Green life floating on top.

I sat on the ground and watched the thick still water lit by a slice of moon. Crickets and cicadas harmonized their tortured strings. I let the blanket drop and the passing breeze sent goose bumps popping across my body. Beside me lay my business cards. Each one read Blake Waterson in bold, strong letters against a bleached white background. If you ran your finger along the card you could feel the raised letters. They were beautiful. One by one I threw the cards into the pool. They landed on the surface, floating on the scum, then sinking away. As I tossed each card, I said my name. Blake Waterson. Each syllable, each letter, again and again. Blake Waterson Blake Waterson Blake Waterson Blake Waterson Blake Waterson Blake Waterson Blake Waterson Blake Waterson BlakeWaterson BlakeWaterson Blakewaters onblakewatersonblakewatersonblakewatersonblakewatersonblakewate rsonblakewatersonblakewatersonblakewatersonblakewatersonblakewa- tersonblakewatersonblakewatersonblakewatersonblakewatersonblake- watersonblakewatersonblakewatersonblakewatersonblakewaterson- blakewatersonblakewatersonblakewatersonblakewatersonblakewater- sonblakewaterson . . .

The sounds ran into each other and finally meant nothing at all . . .

By the time the cards were gone, I no longer had a name. And with my name went all names. I looked at the moon and had no word to call it by. The pool, the lawn, the graves, all nameless. All revealed to be meaningless bumps, imperfections on what should be a flat nothing.

I saw my hands, my bare legs, but I didn't know what they were. Just bumps that should not be. I had no words for thought. Just terror. For a moment I was frozen, unable to move. With names went meaning. With meaning went purpose. I was completely free. I was terrified.

I could have named it all, like Adam in the garden, pointing and naming. But that would be the Fall, the real Fall. Names are lies. Lies are sin. The wages of sin is death.

Already words were trying to sneak back, crawling over the world like flies. Eternity wanted borders. The sky wanted a frame.

I fell back and saw the sky, nameless stars. A plane blinked by. I thought the word: *plane*. And then I was on the plane. I was in the sky with strangers. Flying and flying and flying. The seats and carpet a faded blue—*blue*—almost sky blue. The engine hummed and I leaned my head against the small window and watched the world pass a hundred miles away. Below me was a nameless man by a living pool. Me above me.

The engines stopped, nothing left but a soft whistle. We floated down. The sky was silent and so were we. Terror bled into awe. Here was the end, large and wonderful. The plane melted away, and we were all falling together.

So when someone called out my name, I couldn't hear them.

"Blake."

I was falling.

"Blake," the voice called again. But it was just a noise.

The ground was an instant away.

"Blake Waterson." I looked up, and God was standing in my backyard.

God

God, white light buzzing my eyes, and a voice speaking from the light, giving me back my name.

"Blake. Blake Waterson."

I stood, leaving my blanket, and walked towards the light, towards the Unfathomable, the All. I wept.

"Are you alright?" God said. His voice was a soft woman's voice. Clear, confident, each word well-pronounced.

"We were hoping to ask a few questions." I stopped walking and stared into the light like a dim-witted child gazing at the sun. "You were a follower of Harold Peeks, weren't you?"

God had a microphone, God had a camera.

"Mr. Waterson?" God worked for CNN. "This won't take long. Just a few moments of your time."

And although I realized that this was not God, the awe remained. Standing naked before the omnipotent Creator and standing naked before a world of television viewers is a strikingly similar feeling.

"Sir, is it true you left his church out of protest?"

"My wife died."

I could not turn away. The light had me.

"There are many that claim that much of the violence of the last few weeks is linked to religious hyst—"

"I'm cold."

"Chip, give him your jacket." From the light came clothing. "Many feel that the death of—"

"Death." I was not surprised, but still my heart stumbled.

"Yes," she paused. "Many feel that despite appearances, it was not an accidental death but—"

"They're calling it an accident?"

"Some claim it was intentional."

"It's what Harold wanted."

"So you agree with Bedrick Hobbleton's parents, that Mr. Peeks was negligent and is partially responsible?"

"Bedrick?" I lowered myself to the ground.

"Mr. Waterson?"

"Beddy."

Beddy Is Dead

Beddy was born in Clarkston, California. His parents divorced when he was six. His father moved to New York. Beddy remained with his mother. He played clarinet in the middle school band. At the age of sixteen he moved to New York and lived with his father. He graduated. He traveled. He never attended college. He tried to teach himself guitar. He fell in love at least twice. He collected a bible. He drove and hitchhiked from California to Texas. He met a man who claimed to be the Son of God. He believed him. Beddy died in Austin, Texas.

Harold was preaching in downtown Austin, standing in the bed of a pickup truck, sweating and yelling about that splinter of hope. A crowd watched, a separate crowd stood on the fringes with picket signs and wooden crosses. Traffic passed by, drivers honking and yelling. Someone from the crowd threw a rock, smacking Harold in the head. The news footage shows Harold stumble a little, then catch himself, touch the blood on his forehead, and smile. He is about to say something when the camera moves. There's a scuffle, something is happening, people bump past the camera. You can hear the car's brakes, the sound of impact, but you can't see it. Things clear, the camera pushes forward. Beddy is lying in the road. Irma is holding his hand. Behind her is Shael, eyes of a frightened animal. The driver, a young woman, is screaming. In a moment Harold is kneeling beside Beddy's body.

Some of the protesters cheer and yell out Bible verses. Harold stays very still. He touches Beddy's face. Blood on his fingers. Blood is everywhere. Harold's mouth is moving, but the camera doesn't pick up any of his words.

And there's Beddy, not moving, not breathing. Harold stands. He steps onto the hood of the car that had hit Beddy. Harold raises a foot and with two stomps smashes the windshield in. He turns. No one moves. Even the protestors shut up.

"Judgment is coming," he says in a hoarse voice. "But it will be too late. You'll be dead. You won't even notice." He stares at them all, dangerous eyes. "Don't have any more babies."

He steps off the hood and walks away.

Martyr

In *Harold Be Thy Name*, Beddy pushes a child out of the way of a speeding car and is killed in the process. The child belongs to a redneck woman with a picket sign reading, "Jesus is God's ONLY Son!!!"

There was no child. There was a brief fight, a few pushes. Beddy stepped off the sidewalk at the wrong moment.

What's sad, what knocked Harold out of himself, was that Beddy died for nothing. It was an accident. Pointless. Like a machine breaking. Something changed in Harold. You can see it in the footage, hear it in his words after that day. God had screwed up the story, had killed the wrong person. How could he forgive God for that? Harold's sermons grew sterner. He still spoke of hope, still promised God, but if you were listening you'd notice he never again publicly mentioned the word love. A new doubt edged everything he said. He believed in God, he just didn't trust Him. Eventually, I suppose, all children learn to stop trusting their parents. "I do not know! I do not know!" became his chorus. "The Doubting Messiah," they called him. It was exactly what the world needed. Jesus came to save all those that believe. Harold came for the rest of us.

Don't Have Any More Babies

Harold had been news before Beddy's death. While I was playing hermit, Terry and others had been busy. People all over the country were blogging, twittering, searching Harold Peeks. Hundreds were already swarming to Austin to get a closer look. But it was Beddy's death that made Harold a superstar. His passion was caught on camera. A blurry cell phone video of Beddy's death and Harold's reaction was on the Internet before the body was cold. There were articles, photos. One photo became a classic. Harold kneeling by the body, looking as distraught and as righteously confused as any Old Testament prophet. When it first ran in the *New York Times* it had the caption, "Don't have any more babies."

An Introduction to Haroldism

"Don't Have Any More Babies."

More than one group of Haroldians have interpreted Harold's statement, "Don't have any more babies," as an order not to procreate. They, like the Shakers before them, feel marriage and sex are sinful.

Others claim that the statement was intended only for those who were in the immediate area when the statement was made.

Many lesbian and gay groups feel Harold was pointing out the moral superiority of sex where pregnancy is not possible. Some have gone so far as to proclaim homosexuals God's new Chosen People. One sect of Jewish Haroldian homosexuals describes itself as "the most chosen people on the planet."

Perhaps the most radical and outrageous interpretation of Harold's statement is made by the fringe group, Haroldian Church of Truth and Justice. They argue that Harold's words were misquoted. Instead of saying, "Don't have any more babies," they believe Harold said, "Don't have any Moor babies." According to them, Harold was telling the world to stop birthing black babies. At last count the Haroldian Church of Truth and Justice had over 40,000 members in the United States alone.

The Quote That Saves My Life

I said many things to that reporter in my backyard, that damn light exposing everything, blinding me. She asked. I answered. I only remember bits of what I said. She asked what he was like, what he taught, did he ask for money, why had I followed him? I babbled. I tried to explain, tried to justify why I had left so much for what seemed like so little. Some of my words were full of praise. I spoke of sunrises and rain clouds and the taming of possums. Other words were bitter. My wife died. He did nothing.

Everything I said felt something like lying. Harold doesn't translate. Words don't work. And now here I am over thirty years later, and I'm lying again.

"Do you believe, as many do, that Mr. Peeks, or followers of Mr. Peeks, were responsible for last month's Internet freeze?"

"I'm not sure what . . . Why don't you ask him?"

"Mr. Peeks has refused to be interviewed," she said. "Mr. Waterson, there are those who feel that Mr. Peeks is exploiting the current panic to benefit his own movement. How would you respond to that charge?"

She waited. I watched my toes wriggle.

"Just one more question, Mr. Waterson. Mr. Peeks has grown popular for his insightful comments. Can you tell us, what were Mr. Peeks's wisest words to you?"

"Take your greatest enemy," I said, "the one who stole everything from you and give him a home. Give him food and care, and you will be giving to God."

I don't recall saying it, but I've seen the interview online. The strange thing is, I don't think Harold ever said those words. I made it up. The quote that saves my life. If they knew that I first said those words, would they kill me? Or does it matter anymore?

Today I have taken all the pictures off the wall and the embroidered quote. I've unplugged the lamps and stripped the bed. I've collected all the towels from the bathroom and books from the shelves. I've made a pile in the center of the basement with the Van Gogh print on top. I looked for matches and found I didn't have any. Peter came in with my lunch and saw me sitting cross-legged on the floor in front of my pile. I asked for a match.

"Why?"

I told him I needed to burn some things.

"I can't let you do that."

Never

I wanted to find Steven, find him in his store listening to music I didn't know. I wanted to warn him that nobody promised he'd like what he saw. He wouldn't like Beddy as a corpse or the blood between Harold's fingers or me or a dark blue sky and nowhere to land or broken glass or a pool of water thick with scum. I wanted to find him and warn him and help him. But I never did. Never even tried.

Trust

The morning after the reporter came, I walked out my front door and picked through weeks' worth of newspapers. I spent the day reading.

While I had been hiding in my home, America had popped and was now quickly deflating. Banks had already been failing, companies sinking. That year alone, eight airlines had puttered out. Even Wal-Mart was teetering on bankruptcy. There was also a sort of national guilt as America slowly removed itself from conflicts in which, it was becoming increasingly clear, we had been the bad guy. In February things got worse. The week following Jennifer's funeral, a salmonella outbreak hit the east coast. They blamed lettuce, then beef. By the time they traced it back to mayonnaise, two hundred and twelve people were dead. Toyota announced it would be eliminating its entire American work force, 32,000 jobs. A pipe bomb, built by a group calling itself Americans for a Free Middle East, exploded in a Chicago high school parking lot, killing four. Then, on February 28, the entire Internet froze. No emails, no websites, nothing. America collectively shit itself. After seven panicked hours, the Internet blinked back to life. Computers obediently smiled at their makers as if nothing had happened. More than one group claimed responsibility, but nothing was ever proven and no charges were filed.

The crumble became the Collapse the next day, February 29, Leap Day. It was as if everyone took a long look at that incorporated glitch on the calendar and said, "Ah fuck, there's another thing you can't trust." I've been told you could feel the change like a break in the weather. On that day the market dropped like a dead bird, and somehow everyone knew it would not soar again, not soon at least, not soon enough. Things accelerated. Unemployment, which had already been high, rocketed skyward. The government took emergency action, shoving new money into the economy. But it was just printed paper, and for the first time, Americans saw that. Experts threw out all kinds of terms: a radical drop in investor confidence, a complete paradigm shift in American consumerism, etc. It was simple, really. No one believed in the system anymore, or the government, or the American way of life, and it turned out belief was the only thing that had kept it going.

Beddy died on March 1 and Harold's picture was everywhere. Harold's timing was perfect . . . or the time was perfect for Harold. He showed up just when there was nothing left to believe in.

Lost

The next day, I put on pants and a shirt and climbed into my car. Figwood looked different. Businesses with dark windows, "For Sale" signs in every other front lawn. But my mother-in-law's neighborhood was just as perfect as it had always been. The trees were trimmed, the hedges were immaculately sculpted, and the windows glistened. I rang the doorbell of my mother-in-law's home and listened as the first four notes of some Mozart masterpiece echoed through the house. Then my mother-in-law, dressed in a long-sleeved blue dress and stockings, answered the door.

"Yes?" she asked, as if I were a door-to-door salesman.

"I'd like to speak to Tammy, please."

"You should have called."

"I don't have a phone."

"Dad?" It was Tammy, coming down the stairs with a half-smile. My mother-in-law stepped back and allowed me in. I gave Tammy a hug and we walked to the living room.

I was a mess. Unshowered and unshaven, my hair long and tangled in knots. The house was a bleached white sheet and I was the stain. Everything in and from this home had always been clean and expensive and breakable. I was dirty, of little worth, and very broken.

The air-conditioning filled the house with a dry chill. Too cool to be comfortable. In the living room artificial logs burned away in a gas fireplace.

Tammy and I sat in leather chairs. My mother-in-law kept to the couch, her back straight and her eyes watching me like a mother eagle guarding her eggs from a serpent. I told Tammy how much I missed her and how sorry I was for anything, for everything. Tammy listened to every word but gave no signal about how she felt. I asked if she'd like to come home.

"Well, I don't see how that's possible," my mother-in-law chirped in. "You've got no electricity? You don't have a job."

"We'll get by."

"You have no insurance, no health plan, nothing," she said. "And I don't think Tammy needs the influences of a cult at this point in her life."

"It's not up to you. It's up to Tammy," I said, directing my stare at my daughter. She didn't say anything. She didn't have to. She looked down at her hands and rubbed her knuckles the way her mother used to do. And I knew I was fired.

I nodded. "I guess I'll be going."

They both walked me to the door. But at my car, key in the door, Tammy called out and ran to me.

"Dad," she said, standing a few feet away. "Are you okay?" To see her outside, to see her in morning sunlight, I smiled. My next words surprised me.

"I thought I might be holy," I said.

"Dad?"

"I didn't mean for all this."

"You leave, Dad. You've always been leaving." She stepped closer. "Do you know how old I am?"

"Fifteen."

"I turned sixteen last month."

I shook my head.

"That's okay," she said. "I just wanted you to know I've grown up. And I'm all right."

She thought she was grown up, this little girl in front of me.

"I used to hold you. You were this squirmy little baby. I used to hold you for hours. I used to take care of you."

"I know, Dad. But you can't take care of me anymore." She glanced over at her grandmother standing in the doorway. Then back at me. Right at me. "You need to go home. Sleep some. I'll visit in a few days."

I couldn't talk. The walking, the being alone, the losing. It had cracked any hardness away. Her eyes bruised me. A year before I would've opened the passenger door, stared her down, and demanded she come home. She might not have loved me, but she would have respected me. She would've come home. But I couldn't demand anything of her. Harold had made me weak. She could see it and I could see that she could see it. She loved me. I could see that too. But she pitied me.

"Tammy," her grandmother called. "Time to come in now."

"Daddy, get some sleep, okay?"

I nodded. She leaned up and kissed my cheek. Then she ran back inside.

My daughter has never come to visit me in the Mole Hole. Not even joining her mother to peek in. I watch the vent and wait, but nothing. I imagine she's married. Maybe has some babies. Maybe she's wonderful and happy. Let's just say she's wonderful and happy.

Tonight Is the Night

Peter came in with my breakfast. He was smiling, his eyes shining. He moved around the basement, tidying up and whispering his plan.

"Tonight is the night. Don't do anything different today. Just write and paint. If there's anything you need to take, use the trash bag. Make sure you eat all your meals. You'll need the energy. Late tonight, I'll come back. It will be dark. The whole place will be. The power will be out, but it will only last a few minutes, then the generators kick in. We have to be outside before that happens or the alarms will sound. Get some rest but try not to sleep too deeply. Do you understand, Mr. Waterson?"

Today of All Days

I left my mother-in-law's house intending to drive home, sit in my kitchen, and put a bullet into my forehead. Last time my nerve had failed me. But I just needed the right motivation. My daughter's eyes had provided that. I sincerely wanted to die. Quickly.

When I pulled into my driveway, I found Terry sitting on my doorstep. He had a box of fried chicken beside him and was wearing a black shirt with bold white type saying, "ASK ME ABOUT HAROLD."

"Blake, it's good to see you. You look good."

I did not acknowledge him.

"I saw your interview on the CNN. Heavy stuff. Nice to see you with some pants on," he chuckled, slapping my back. "I was on MSNBC. Did you see it?"

I wanted to get inside and kill myself. I tried to maneuver around him, but Terry blocked my path.

"Don't ignore me, Blake," he said, his face turning stern. "It's time to end the pity party. Harold needs you."

"Harold needs me?"

"He needs all of us. Today of all days. After the announcement, things will—"

"What announcement?"

He stared at me for a long moment. "Have you heard nothing? Today, in Austin! Harold's giving his first press conference. Says he's going to announce something."

"Announce what?"

"Well, it seems pretty obvious to me. I mean, can't you just feel it? He's going to tell them, tell everyone who he really is!"

My stomach bubbled. "Who is he, Terry?"

"God, of course. God in the flesh!" His hands sprang towards me as if he were flinging water from his fingers. "You, of all people, should know that. We are blessed, Blake. We've known him since the start. We were there when the fire was lit! And you, you walked with him! With God! Like the twelve, right? Now, I don't know why he sent you away, but that's all—"

"Sent me away?"

Terry dropped his hands and met my eyes. "Well, didn't he?"

I pushed past him into my house and slammed the door, late morning shadows scuttling to corners. This was my home, this pit where madness stained the air like the stench of wet ash. Harold as God was too much for me to take. The truth is at some point I might have accepted it, might have cheered and ranted like Terry outside my door. But now . . . If Harold is God then God let my wife die. If Harold is God then God was unable to save Beddy. If Harold is God then God is too weak and too cruel for me stomach. I found my pistol, but I didn't put it to my head. Instead I walked back out the front door.

"It's okay," Terry said. "He sent me away too. It's okay. It's not about you or me or anybody. It's about Harold, the movement! Ri—"

I grabbed his shirt and shoved the pistol into his mouth until he gagged. He tried to shake away, almost a spasm, but I held firm, the barrel shaking against his teeth.

"Terry," I said, my voice weird to my ears. "Never talk to me again."

He had tears in his eyes. He moaned. I removed the gun, walked to my car, and drove away. The last I saw of Terry was in my rearview mirror, sitting on my front porch, his head between his knees.

Billions of Words

You cannot drive to where you once walked. The journey changes the destination. I was driving to Austin. But it was not the same Austin.

The road was filled with pilgrims, new eager followers. Walking, many of them, as I had walked, except they were near the highway. Some were singing, dancing. Others were somber, walking with their heads lowered. And there were the opponents as well, more and more the closer I got to Austin. Billboards and posters crying out that Harold was not to be trusted, idols were not to be worshipped, Jesus was the truth, hell was waiting. I honked and waved at all of them.

Every newsbreak on every station focused on either Harold or the Collapse. Those were the two stories. The economy is imploding. The Messiah is arriving.

Talk radio was insane. Stories about Harold having several wives and dozens of children. Harold demanding sex from his followers. Harold having millions of dollars hidden in secret bank accounts. One man came forward swearing Harold had killed his mother.

And the sightings. People called in and swore on-air that Harold was in a yogurt shop in Pensacola, Florida, a subway in New York City, a children's hospital in Wichita, Kansas. Suddenly anyone could claim Harold.

Reporters rattled off any Harold fact they could find: where he went to high school, how much he paid in taxes, what charities he had given to.

There was never a shortage of facts about Harold. We hardly know anything about Jesus of Nazareth. Just odds and ends. We're left to piece together a picture from hand-me-down rewrites and a few fading words on scraps of parchment. The picture is underexposed, all shadow and black. But with Harold the opposite is true. To find Harold you have to dig through an unending pile of information and misinformation. By now, there are billions of words written about Harold. Hardly any of them are worth the letters it took to spell them. The picture is overexposed, all white. He is lost.

Beddy's death made Harold popular, but his own death made him divine. Death took Harold out of time. Allowed us to experience him as we experience God. He could be all over the place at once. Not just random sightings, but personal, private experiences. "He's with us now," they'd say. "Harold is in our hearts."

Little factions within churches started to pop up within a year of his death. Pockets of Christians who believed Harold was the Second Coming or at least a prophet. Terry's web page church became one of many. Some Jewish groups believed Harold was the Messiah finally come. A faction of Muslims claimed he was Abu al-Qasim Muhammad, the Hidden Imam. And many others who had had no faith before found it in Harold. These groups began meeting together in a series of conferences, dozens of conferences, trying to decide what Harold had meant. Harold had talked about throwing out rules. Now they met to make rules on how to throw out the rules. How to experience what Harold was. How to still the water so everyone can have a sip without getting too wet.

Each conference led to splits. More rules. More attempts to clear up the mystery. Harold never wanted to clear up any mystery. Harold would have hated that. He embraced ignorance. The only answer he provided was that you don't need answers. But Harold's not around to argue. Or if he is, he's not saying anything.

Wake Up

I lay on my cot fully dressed waiting for Peter. I massaged my legs so they would be ready to run. Once I was free from this basement, I'd head south again. Mexico didn't work last time. I stayed still for too long, had to deal with those damn painted prayers. So I headed back north, crossed the Rio Grande again, sneaking back home. That didn't work either.

This time I'd go further south. South enough for the world to turn strange. Find a place where the images are as foreign as the language, where facial expressions mean nothing to me. I want a world where no one can reach me. So far south the sky is liquid and the ocean is air. *Get lonely enough and God meets you there.*

At some point I closed my eyes and slept. When I opened them again it was dark. My heart froze. Where was I? I blinked. I could not see a thing. It was so dark my closed eyes seemed to see more.

"Mr. Waterson," I heard Peter call from somewhere and I remembered. "Mr. Waterson, wake up." There was a weight to that darkness. It covered my body. Held me against the cot. "Mr. Waterson." His voice was urgent. "Now, Mr. Waterson. We have to go right now." I heard other voices, loud and angry. Yes. Now. Move body. Go. But my body did not go. I was too frightened to move, to speak. Not afraid of my captors, but afraid of losing them. Afraid of being free again.

"Mr. Waterson, please. The generators. The alarm. Please." Other steps, fast steps. I held my breath. Run, Peter. They're coming! Run! I can't move. The black like a lead blanket. "Mr. Waterson. Mr. Waterson!"

Closed

When the lights came back on minutes later, the door was closed and I was alone. I heard muffled yelling and more steps. Then everything went quiet. I lay awake for hours. Not moving until a knock came from the door and an older man walked in with my breakfast on a tray.

"Where's Peter?" I asked.

He placed the tray down and said nothing. His eyes darted from side to side.

"It was my fault," I said. "Where is he?"

He was sweating. He moved quickly. The door clicked closed behind him.

Peter, what did they do to you?

Dies

No lunch. No dinner. No face peeking through the door's window. Not a sound. They've left me to die.

I'm writing from my cot. If I had the strength I could fill the bathtub and finish the job. But I wouldn't, even if I could. How do you die? Still don't know.

Piece by piece this boat is falling apart. My weak limbs, my weak mind, my weak voice. This boat is sinking. I suppose the boat has to sink or I would never choose to swim. Even when it sinks I might not swim. I could drown scraping at the boards of a boat that was never designed to last this long.

Doesn't a fetus think it's dying? Its gills fade away, it can't move, it feels the pressure pushing it out of its world. It must think the end has come.

Even my memory fades. It's not a time for memory. Everything is telling me to look forward, to lose the old eyes so I may gain the new. But I don't. I hate the blackness. Why should I hope there is any good, or anything at all beyond that black? So I'm clinging to the sides of the womb.

Go to the black and don't come back.

I wish Beddy were here. I wish he would slip through my vent and sit with me. Maybe he'd tell me a story. Ramble like he always did. Tell me about the aquarium in Monterey where he worked for a summer.

"Yes, yes, there's the blue in those waters," he tells me. "Like the water is making its own light. And all those fish and crawlers and floaters and things I would have sworn were made up by a child, like sea horses and jellyfish."

"Maybe that's it," I say. "Maybe God's just a five-year-old."

"Maybe on the fourth day God created mushrooms, got high, and that afternoon he made all this." He laughs and his bangs fall over his eyes. "Nice. Nice to see reality a few steps ahead of my imagination. Gives me hope."

But he won't come anymore.

If you move not forward from silence or backward from silence, but downward into silence, then the moment of silence is an abyss.

Instead, my daughter's cat comes. The mother of the kittens I drowned. Her rusty fur is sticky and clotted. She tells me she's come to watch me die. She doesn't seem angry, doesn't hiss or scratch at me. Just curls up on my chest as I lay on the cot.

"Does my daughter miss me?" I ask her.

Not in a painful way.

I'm sorry about your children.

I'm sorry about yours.

"Please tell her I love her."

Of course.

Waterson Fires; Peeks Falls

It had not rained in nineteen days. No clouds, no gray, just the blue sky stoically refusing the earth any relief. Back in Figwood, men were holding hoses over brown grass, praying for rain and resurrection. But the sky held its breath, and the ground dried up like dead skin. Then, on the day I drove to Austin, on the day Harold died, the sky exhaled and the rains came.

Hours of water, pouring down like revenge. Hot rain. I didn't mind it. I abandoned the car blocks from the middle school where the press conference was being held. The rain soaked through my shirt and pants. It dripped from my shaggy hair and beard. All the world was wet. The gun was heavy in my pocket. I had no plan. My brain was fire and no thought, and the rain did nothing to douse it.

The school was surrounded with open-mouthed gawkers, wide-eyed wanters—the masses.

I pushed my way through. "Harold, Harold," they mumbled and moved closer to touch me. They thought I was him. And why not? There weren't many good photos. We both were unkempt. My face, like his, was covered with a month's worth of beard. I looked like Jim Morrison, John Lennon, Charles Manson. I looked liked Jesus. I looked like Harold.

Closer to the school, the press stood guard. Pretty people with umbrellas, vans with antennas, cameras, and microphones. All sucking images and noises. I did not like them.

The rain was just slowing to a drizzle as I walked in to the school with a small crowd of reporters and photographers. I stood with them in the back of the cafeteria. In front of the room was a low stage. Irma and Shael were already sitting down. Gilbert showed up soon after. Of course he came back. Of course. They were all dry and clean. I loved them very much. No one saw me behind the cameras.

The press had set up a long table for Harold and the others to sit at. They took their places facing the reporters. This time it was the Last Supper.

Harold came last. He was as hairy and wet as me, wearing his red poncho and dripping water onto the floor. *Bzzz* and *whzzz*, went the press. There was no smile left on his face. He looked older, and there was a heaviness in his eyes. He moved to the center of the table, touching

Shael's shoulder. I hated him. I hated how lonely I was. He taught me how to feel and then gave me more pain than I'd ever known.

He opened his mouth to talk. Then stopped. He saw me. His eyes fixed on my eyes. He smiled. I smiled. That moment. That quiet. For an instant it seemed possible that only I could see him. This was a vision, and only for me.

"Blake?" Shael said. The quiet was gone.

"Holy crap! Blake!" Gilbert yelled.

Then they turned on me. Lights and lenses. Harold jumped from the stage and came to me. I was shaking, my hand resting on the pistol. Harold was close now. Smiling. I started to cry.

Following him cost me my daughter. But that is not why I fired. He let my wife die. But that's not why I fired. He gave me as much doubt as he gave me faith. But that's not why I fired. I would have dropped all my anger and embraced him then and there. I would have taken my place at the table, but I saw his eyes. The truth is he wanted me to pull the trigger. It was the one thing I could do for him. I fired.

Shael yelling, Gilbert tackling me, police pushing my head to the ground, then solid blackness.

But the cameras sucked on.

The video footage is famous. The trampling out of the room. The crowd outside yelling and crying as the news rippled through it, *Harold has been shot.* TVs in cars, TVs on cameras, TVs on phones all showed the event over and over. Me shooting, Harold falling. Me shooting, Harold falling. Harold, a martyred saint on a billion screens. *Can anyone see any blood? How bad was the wound? He's wearing red, we can't tell. Show it again, show it again. Slow motion, different angle. 3-D graphics. Waterson fires; Peeks falls.*

An ambulance arrives, splashing through puddles. The cameras filmed the attendants squeezing through the crowd and into the school building. They return carrying a stretcher between the two of them.

Oh, God, it's Harold. His face. Oh, God, look at the blood.

And his chest, It's all blood.

No, no. It's water. It's just the red poncho.

The crowd and the cameras weep and wave goodbye as they load the body into the ambulance.

One attendant rushes back into the school. In a moment the doors opened and the cameras hiss.

The footage shows a hurt man held up by an attendant and police officer. He stumbles. He might run. The crowd pounces. The camera follows as they knock the police officer away and grab me. The body bouncing above the crowd, thrown back, finally falling to the cement. Fists and kicking and all I deserve. More yelling and kicking and all America playing along at home, watching my face in a puddle. They're holding me there in the water. More kicks to my side, to the back, to the groin, and my face is still in the puddle. One man puts his foot on my head and pushes down. The puddle is red, I struggle, but I'm held and then I stop moving. The cameras are there when they roll me over and see that Harold is dead.

I had watched the whole event from the ambulance. I watched them beat and kill Harold thinking it was me.

What happened? I remember being knocked down by Gilbert inside the school. I remember the gun being pulled from my hands. I remember being hit in the head until my vision went black. Then I remember coming to and seeing Harold sitting by me on the school floor. His face was red with blood, Shael holding a towel against the side of his head. Shael looked at me only once. It hurt more than Gilbert's tackle.

"You're in shock," Harold said to me and placed his red poncho around my shoulders. The red poncho that the crowds knew as his.

"But I . . ." my mouth felt thick. It was difficult to form words. "I shot you?"

"I think you shot my ear. Hurts like hell," he said. Shael readjusted the towel. Harold winced, then smiled. "Who knew you were such a bad shot?"

"I'll do better next time," I mumbled.

"Blake," he said softly, blood streaming down his face. "I have nothing but love for you. That's sort of a miracle, isn't it?"

The ambulance attendants arrived and lifted me on to a stretcher. Harold stayed beside me, a hand on my chest. Shael went for more towels and for a moment, we were alone.

"Thank you," he said.

"For shooting you?"

"No," he laughed. I tried to concentrate, to stay awake, but I could feel the blackness rising. "I understand now. At least a little," he said, his face fading. "I'm not the only one who will suffer for their sins."

Nothing but black.

They carried me out on a stretcher and the world, seeing Harold's red poncho, thought I was Harold. The attendant and the police officer were helping Harold leave the school. The blood covering his face like a mask. And the crowds grabbed him. I was in the ambulance, my brain aching. I heard the screaming and looked. From my spot crouching by the ambulance, I couldn't see Harold's face, only the faces watching his. Faces as they realized it was not me they had beaten. They dropped, they twisted. The attendants who had carried me from the school ran to Harold's side. But I knew from the faces that Harold was dead.

I ran.

I ran. Back behind the cars and vans and trucks with the cameras and televisions. They hid me from the crowd. Then I was across the street and into the woods where the mosquitoes buzzed in my face.

I ran until I fell. I wanted to cry out and die. But I did neither. Instead I thought: How can I hide?

I was soaking wet, muddy water dripping from my hair and my beard and soon, very soon, I was going to have the world hunting me.

The rain started to fall again, and I thanked God for it. It would cover my tracks. I kept running along the creek, trying to think, but coming up with nothing. I slipped in the mud and slid into the creek, swallowing a stomach full of dirty water. Stuck in the branches of a fallen tree, I saw a plastic children's pool, the kind you buy for a summer and throw away in the fall. I tugged it free, turned it over, and hid under it. It was dark under that shell and my breaths echoed. But it worked. I floated past houses and lawns. I floated under bridges. Above me the police were checking each car.

Most of the time I could touch the bottom of the creek and push myself along. When it got deep, I held on to the sides of the pool and let the current carry me. Often it was so shallow I had to stick my legs out in front of me. Hours went by and I was exhausted, but I kept going. The water soaked through me, past my clothes, past my skin, into my bones and deeper still. After night fell, I crawled out, lay on the creek's bank, and immediately slept. I was too tired to dream.

I woke up shivering. It was still dark. I abandoned the pool and made my way out of the woods, past suburban houses and strip malls. A drop-off box at a thrift store provided some dry clothes, and I slept another hour behind a dumpster. When I opened my eyes again, the sky was that pale blue.

My body was dry, but my mind had soaked up too much mud. I started walking. I had nowhere to go and was too dazed to care. I had no wallet and no food.

The streets were already filled with cars waiting in line to get to work. I stood on the corner, no longer trying to hide, and wondered which car would recognize me first. Would it be the Escort, or the minivan or that blue SUV? Who would dial 911 and report that Judas was tramping through their neighborhood?

The light turned green, the cars crawled past. But the SUV paused. A hand reached out from the half-lowered, tinted window with a twenty-dollar bill. I grabbed the money, and the SUV drove on.

My minded cleared. I was hungry. More hungry than I had ever been, but I knew that food was not what I needed most. I needed a haircut. I walked for less than a mile and found a dingy barbershop. Inside a tiny man greeted me in Spanish. I told him I didn't understand and motioned my requests. He sat me down and snipped away my hair and shaved my face. He spoke Spanish the entire time and I nodded along.

In less than fifteen minutes, I was a new man. I handed him my twenty dollars and he handed me eight dollars in change.

I left and walked past a newspaper dispenser. There I was on the front page. The long-haired, scruffy-bearded me. Not the clean-shaven, short-haired me. I read half a page through the plastic window. It was already clear, the crowd had killed Harold but I was the one to blame. I had fired the shot. I was the focus of the anger. They laid their sins upon me.

At a convenience store I bought a package of Twinkies and a Coke. I sat in the parking lot and took my communion. This is my body . . . a yellow sponge. This is my blood . . . sweet, black, and bubbly.

What now? What now? What now? What now?

Simple, really. The play had already been written. I was to buy a field or throw my thirty pieces of silver somewhere and hang myself or let my intestines spill out or something like that. But I had just spent most of my silver on a haircut and some Twinkies, so instead I did what he had taught me to do. I walked.

All that day I walked, and days more. There was no resurrection, but just as Harold had predicted, people waited. His body was placed under twenty-four hour police guard. Even after his burial at Onion Creek Memorial Park, just south of Austin, converts flocked to his grave in hopes of witnessing a miracle. Only Shael was brave enough to attempt Harold's request. She was arrested breaking into the cemetery in the dead of night with a shovel and two jugs of gasoline.

She was quickly denounced as a traitor. Not quite as bad as me, but in the same category. Her mother paid her bail and she disappeared.

An Introduction to Haroldism

Self-Examination

A healthy amount of self-doubt has long been a virtue of the Haroldian movement. Believers need only think of Blake Waterson and Shael Weil to be reminded how quickly a seemingly devote follower can fall into betrayal. By many accounts, no one was closer to Harold Peeks in his adult life than Shael Weil, yet she was charged with attempting to desecrate his grave. Her reasons are a mystery, but her actions, like the actions of Blake Waterson, illustrate to Haroldians that outward devotion is never a guarantee of inner stability and faith. Believers are encouraged to examine and reexamine their hearts to weed out the envy and pride that can so quietly poison the spiritual life.

Stop Salvation

I walked. All that year and years more.

I walked all over. False names and part-time work. I went north and east. Years and years I walked as Haroldism blossomed around me. Shael never reappeared. Irma died. Gilbert died. I lived on the streets, in shelters or flop hotels with cheap weekly rates. I snuck into Mexico and lived in a cinderblock shack. I walked and grew old. I found myself standing above the oily waters of a reservoir under a single fluorescent light.

Those rainbows, catching white light and shattering it. This was my Field of Blood. And it occurred to me, while standing above the water, that perhaps there would still be a resurrection, that Harold might return to save us all. I was still alive, so the story was stalled. How could Jesus rise from the dead while Judas was still around? If I loved Harold, if I loved any soul, then I must jump. I was holding back salvation.

"You don't have to jump into the water. Just jump into the air. Gravity will do the rest."

Then the Pastels came.

"Mr. Waterson, we've come to help you."

I jumped. I let myself sink down into the cold blackness. Come on Harold, hold me down. I could hear them jump in after me. I tried to suck the water in.

Save me and you'll stop salvation. Stop resurrection.

An Introduction to Haroldism
Second Baptism

The second baptism of the Haroldian year takes place on Stones Throw, which is traditionally celebrated on April 18. Stones Throw marks the end of a month of mourning after the anniversary of Harold's death. Haroldians take this month to meditate on conviction and guilt. This prepares the faithful for the Celebration of Grace beginning on April 19.

Stones Throw is invariably linked to the crimes of Blake Waterson. It was on this day that police discovered the red rain poncho in which Blake Waterson was last seen. The poncho was floating in Lady Bird Lake near the Shoal Creek tributary in Austin, Texas. Though no body was ever found, this discovery led many to believe that Blake Waterson took his life just days or weeks after the death of Harold. Others argue he is still at large.

On the morning of Stones Throw, Haroldians find a midsized stone and carry it with them in their pocket or purse. Throughout the day, they confess to the stone their sins, pains, and struggles. At sunset, believers gather near any local body of water. They then turn to one another and say:

"I am Blake. Forgive me."

And answer each other:

"I am Harold. You are forgiven."

Believers then cast their stones into the body of water and state the following:

"I drown as Blake, for I am Blake.
I live as Harold, for I am Harold.
Let me give to God."

Weather permitting, believers then participate in a brief swim. Otherwise, a bath or shower is adequate.

Today

That's it. That's what I remember. That's my confession.

Hours pass in the Mole Hole with me on my back tracing the corners of the room with my eyes. Still no one. I haven't eaten in over a day. I've moved past hunger. My body feels light, as if it might float, but I cannot move. My breaths are shallow and full of scratch. The sheets are wet from my sweat and urine.

I'm sleeping when the noises start, and the sounds clang into my dreams, above me, through the ceiling. Yells. Breaking glass, words I can't make out. My eyes are open, but it still feels like a dream. Noises now outside my door. It continues for a few minutes, and then with a crack like a bat snapping in two, my door flies open and four men and a girl pour in. They're young. Their eyes are young. One of them is Peter.

Peter is beside me, kneeling, grinning. I squeeze his hand.

"I'm sorry," I say, but he's talking and doesn't hear me.

"We're taking you out of here, Mr. Waterson. They can't keep you locked up. We're taking you away."

"Last night . . ."

"I ran. I called the news, I called churches, everyone. Hundreds of people are here, just outside. Maybe a thousand."

"No. No. They'll hurt me." My breath is almost gone. "Please don't . . ."

He puts a hand on my head and I want to cry. "You're the last of his followers, Mr. Waterson. The last one. After you, all we have is words. No one will hurt you."

The other men and the girl pick up my cot and lift me to their shoulders. I sway in midair, the ceiling a close sky. It's happening so fast, but I have no breath to protest. They carry me up the stairs, heads bobbing by my side, the pretty girl smiling at me. We walk through the church. I see some of the Pastels standing at a distance looking sheepish. Looking afraid.

As we reach the doors to the outside, I put up a hand. "Wait," I ask between gasps. "Let me stop and write for a moment."

The young people place my cot on the ground. Peter kneels beside me, a hand on my chest. I'm afraid. He nods. When did I become a child?

Over my wheezing, I can hear the crowds outside, like ocean waves. They will touch me. They will pass me over their heads, over the crowd, floating over all them.

I will see the sky. I am not afraid. Sky above, people below. I will bless them all even if they kill me. I will tell them the whole world is wet with God. Like I want my next breath. That's all. It took me all these years to breathe and be blessed. It's this breath. The one you are taking right now.

Acknowledgments

This novel would never have come to be if not for the friends, family, colleagues, and instructors who read and re-read my pages and offered wise words of guidance and encouragement. The list would fill another book, but allow me to at least thank Nancy Thomas, Russell and Cheryl Sharman, the faculty and my fellow students at Texas State University, and, of course, Jodi Egerton—my sweet, patient love. My kids, Arden and Oscar, didn't read a word of this book, but they never fail to inspire. I owe a huge bulging bag of gratitude to Deltina Hay and the gang at Dalton Publishing for pushing this book to print. And my heart breaks into operatic praise for the editing, encouragement, talent, and friendship of Stacey Swann.

Thanks to Adam Lindsay Gordon (1833-1870) and his poem "Ye Wearie Wayfarer," from which this novel quotes.